Ethel Sturges Dummer
A Pioneer of American Social Activism

Ethel M. Lichtman

iUniverse, Inc.
New York Bloomington

iUniverse books may be ordered through booksellers or by contacting:

iUniverse
1663 Liberty Drive
Bloomington, IN 47403
www.iuniverse.com
1-800-Authors (1-800-288-4677)

Because of the dynamic nature of the Internet, any Web addresses or links contained in this book may have changed since publication and may no longer be valid. The views expressed in this work are solely those of the author and do not necessarily reflect the views of the publisher, and the publisher hereby disclaims any responsibility for them.

ISBN: 978-1-4401-7056-0 (sc)
ISBN: 978-1-4401-7057-7 (ebook)

Printed in the United States of America

iUniverse rev. date: 9/25/2009

Cover Photo: Ethel Sturgest Dummer with her daughters Marion and Katherine, 1894.

Contents

Note to Researchers

This book was researched and written over the space of a decade by Ethel Mintzer Lichtman as a work of love and respect for her grandmother, Ethel Sturges Dummer. During this period, the author received a great deal of advice and help from a number of sources, including family and academic professionals with an interest in the life and times of Ethel Sturges Dummer.

As fate would have it, the author completed the manuscript in the middle of 2008; within a very short period of time following completion she suffered what may have been a mild stroke that significantly impaired memory function. She was therefore unable to be involved in the final editing and publication of the book.

Knowing that she was committed to completing this retrospective of the work of her grandmother's life, and honoring the moral and financial support of members of the extended family, I have undertaken to have the work published. I was not able to re-visit the many sources of information that she had compiled, or to check footnotes or any other citations for accuracy. We do know that the vast majority of the sources used for this work are housed in the Ethel Sturges Dummer Collection at the Schlesinger Library, Radcliffe Institute for Advanced Study, Harvard University. Interested parties are invited to direct their attention towards this authoritative collection and asked to forgive the author for any inaccuracies that may remain.

Grant Lichtman,
2009

I. The Early Years: 1866-1920

Growing Up

On October 8, 1871, when Ethel Sturges Dummer was five years old, a small fire in a soon to become infamous Chicago barn grew into a huge conflagration that raged for thirty hours and burned over 18,000 buildings. The family home, built by Ethel's grandfather, Solomon Sturges and said to be one of the finest in Chicago,[1] was on the corner of Pine (later North Michigan Avenue) and Huron Streets a few blocks from Lake Michigan. It burned to the ground. The family fled by train to Lake Geneva, Wisconsin, where Ethel's father had recently purchased a summer home. For the less fortunate, Ethel later told her grandchildren, one of the Sturges servants took the family cow down to the lake and milked it for children who had fled there with their families to escape the flames.

Ethel had been born in 1866 into one of Chicago's most affluent families. Her father, George Sturges, was president of the Northwestern National Bank, a building that was also largely destroyed in the fire. After the fire, many banks were in doubt about the status of their bills receivable and uncertain what course to pursue in dealing with

---

1   Solomon Sturges and His Descendents - A Memoir and a Genealogy, (hereafter called Sturges Memoir)compiled by Ebenezer Buckingham; The Grafton Press, New York, MCMVII. Solomon Sturges 1796-1864, from Putnam (later Zanesfield) Ohio, moved to Chicago in 1855. He built a grain warehouse that stored a quarter of the grain that passed through the city; owned grain-carrying vessels on the Great Lakes and tugboats in Chicago; and had extensive business interests in Illinois and nearby states. In 1880 he established the banking firm of Sturges and Sons.

depositors. George Sturges and Chauncy Blair of the Merchants Bank boldly announced their intention to open their doors and meet all their liabilities on demand, whether other banks did or not. "It required courage to take this stand at such a time, but it added to the reputation of the two men, and the results amply justified the wisdom of the course they advocated." [2]

In 1862 George Sturges had married Mary Delafield of Memphis, Tennessee, who was seventeen years younger than her husband. She was a member of the large Delafield family, descended from John Delafield who first arrived in New York City in 1783. She was a woman of rare strength and personal charm, deeply attached to her husband and exercising a strong influence on him. [3]

The Sturgeses had nine children, seven of whom survived to adulthood. Ethel was the eldest of five daughters. While the bank building and their Chicago home were being rebuilt after the fire, the family lived in the small home Ethel's father had purchased as a summer home in Lake Geneva. After the Chicago fire, George Sturges bought more property surrounding their Lake Geneva house. It became their permanent home until their new home in Chicago was completed. (In 1894 Mrs. Sturges donated this building and property to the City of Lake Geneva with the stipulation that it be used as a public park and library. A modern brick building has replaced the wooden structure that served as the first George Sturges Lake Geneva home.) In 1882 the Sturgeses moved into a much larger summer home on the Lake which they named "Snug Harbor". Far from being "snug", the three-story mansion resembled a French Chateau, with castle-like qualities including a five-story tower. The growing family loved their Lake Geneva home. Snug Harbor was opened each year as soon as warm weather appeared. Other members of the Sturges family were also building large homes in Lake Geneva. [4]

In her autobiography written in 1935, Ethel describes a childhood and girlhood spent alternating between winters in Chicago and summers at

---

2   Ibid

3   Ibid

4   Ann Wolfmeyer and Mary Burns Gage, <u>Lake Geneva, Newport of the West, 1870-1920, Vol I</u>, pp. 18 & 19, Copyright 1976, Lake Geneva Historical Society.

Lake Geneva, with occasional trips to the East Coast and Europe. The Sturges children's lives were enriched with every joy that could be given by thoughtful parents. The children were accustomed to hospitality. Ethel's father and mother were the ones turned to by others of their families for guidance, assistance and fun. Whole families visited at a time. At Lake Geneva the children had horses and row boats; the boys later had sailboats. George Sturges had a steam yacht, and the family spent evenings on the water, always taking groups of neighbors. The Sturges children drove about the country roads with their cousins in a surrey, singing at the top of their voices, climbed hills, played in the lake and picked wildflowers in the woods. Their mother encouraged them to make their own festivities. As the eldest Sturges daughter, Ethel recalls, social responsibilities came to her early, especially during two long illnesses of her mother's when she had to take her place at the table. "In trying to do my duty I fear I was giving free rein to my ego in dominating, for years later one who had lived near us as a child told someone that I had been a martinet. In my effort properly to carry out the duties of elder sister, I must have been a pest." [5]

At an early age, Ethel had a keen awareness of the differences between the sexes. Expectations and opportunities afforded boys and girls from the youngest age were widely divergent. She illuminates her recognition of this disparity in her autobiography. After being allowed to climb trees with the boys during childhood, her father soon reminded her that girls wore dresses and she must give up climbing. She was envious of her brothers with their sailor suits and caps that they wore when they were on the water.

In their younger years, the Sturges children were tutored at home. They all had a natural love of studying. As they grew, their schooling showed Ethel another disparity between boys' and girls' upbringing. When Ethel reached adolescence, she attended The Kirkland School, a private preparatory school in Chicago, run by Miss Elizabeth Kirkland. Looking back in her autobiography, Ethel remembers Miss Kirkland who taught history and literature, and Mrs. E. S. Adams who taught science

5   Ethel S. Dummer, Why I Think So - The Autobiography of an Hypothesis, pp. 10-12; 1937, Clarke-McElroy Publishing Company, Chicago; hereafter referred to as Dummer Book.

and mathematics, as teachers unsurpassed in that day. Nevertheless, she noticed that the textbooks used by her brothers at St. Paul's School in New Hampshire seemed far superior to hers. One brother made the highest marks that had ever been given in his grade. Ethel said later that her unconscious jealousy of her brothers' opportunities may have been a source of her later feminism. [6]

The combined religious thinking of Ethel's parents was an important influence on developing the young girl's spiritual thinking, what she later referred to as the "inner philosophic me". Her religious philosophy was shaped by the church-going activities of her parents. During her early years, for example, a man named David Swing was expelled from the pulpit of the nearby Presbyterian Church because he did not believe in infant damnation. Ethel's father, though not a regular church-goer, helped to rent a large music hall in which Professor Swing preached for years to large audiences. The older Sturges children and their mother alternated between the Episcopal service and the "thrilling independent thinker" to whom her father listened each Sunday. The combination of the beautiful English ritual and the free thinker, with open discussion at home, provided a stimulating religious environment and influence.[7]

Mary Delafield Sturges brought up her children according to the principles of the Christian Golden Rule and the Sermon on the Mount. Her religion was not dogmatic theology, but more a daily attempt to follow New Testament teachings. She kept by her bedside a set of tiny religious and philosophical books, which Ethel felt were "life preservers" during her mother's busy years. The books covered selections from *Ecclesiastics* and Epictetus, Plato's *Phaedo* and *Apology*, Marcus Aurelius, Thomas a Kempis's *Imitation of Christ* and a selection of poems entitled *Sunshine in the Soul*. Ethel not only read them to her mother, but recalled later that she must have devoured them, for at eighteen she bought the set for herself.

At the Kirkland School Ethel's teachers emphasized the social service obligations of wealthy women. [8] She describes her years there as a source

---

6   Ibid. p.10
7   [5]Ibid. pp. 5-8
8   Dummer Book, pp. 14-17

of awakening experience, as having an important influence on her life. She remembered the experience later as the basis of her integrated approach to learning, which became central to educating herself and others throughout her life. She believed her teachers were exceptional in their knowledge of subjects and in their ability to teach. An example she cites of an event at school, however, seems more indicative of her own persistence than of her teachers' ability. It also illustrates a theme of the interrelation of subjects that became central to her later thinking.

In her junior year at age seventeen, astronomy, plane trigonometry and logic, all taught by Mrs. E. S. Adams, was a fascinating combination of courses for Ethel. One day something special happened. Ethel had worked and worked on a problem of trigonometry at the back of the book. A night's sleep, which at times had helped solve algebraic problems, proved unproductive. Having no more time to give it the next day, she turned to astronomy. Opening the book, there was the "sidereal distance" (relating to stars or constellations) upon which she had been working the previous day, with <u>her</u> answer, not the one given in the textbook. Suddenly all the pigeonholes of knowledge broke down for her. No longer were trigonometry, astronomy and logic separated; they all seemed to merge. She saw history, language, literature, science - the past, present and future, all fusing into a vast whole. This was a revelation in Ethel's mind. In her later memory of this incident, she had come to see the whole world as a unity, with life in its space-time relationship. This insight became a reference for all that came later in her reading, observation, and experience. When Einstein's ideas of space-time relativity burst upon the world, she realized she had needed them. Mathematically, of course, she knew they were out of her field, but they met a philosophic need. When she first referred to Einstein, an academic told her that this was not at all what Einstein meant. [9][14]

In 1885, at age nineteen, Ethel gave the commencement address at The Kirkland School. Many of her comments reveal her developing theory about women in history up to and including that time. For centuries women were mere slaves, she told the audience. Religion,

---

9 [14] <u>Notable American Women: The Modern Period; A Biographical Dictionary</u> edited by Barbara Sicherman and Carol Hurd Green; Radcliffe College, Harvard University Press; 1980; p. 208

education, and literature were withheld from them. It remained for the glorious nineteenth century to give them liberty. After having risen to the height which a woman has attained, she added, it "certainly does not seem just that she should still be classed in the law respecting voting with minors and idiots."

The young Ethel believed that the education of her sex should develop a lofty ideal of womanhood, making her a "real woman" and not a poor imitation of a man. She viewed most women as shrinking from publicity and association with the "under classes" which active participation in community life would necessitate. But she saw others smothering these feelings, taking up the causes of women's rights, "believing that in this way only may (women's) wrongs be redressed, and that their voices in government might save their fellow sisters from much sorrow and suffering. If education were merely for our pleasure", her address continued, "it would have been unnecessary, for not knowing what hidden treasures were within our reach, we should have been happy in our ignorance and missed nothing. But with each taste of knowledge comes a corresponding responsibility, a certain debt which must be paid by sharing the benefit derived therefrom with others, and using the learning acquired to aid and instruct fellow workers". [1015]

Ethel saw Christianity, teaching love and charity, as essential attributes of a true woman, placing her on a higher plane than she had reached before. It seemed to her that these virtues should form the steps by which women could climb to a "higher life". With Christianity as the foundation and education the means, a higher life was open to all women. She embroidered a favorite saying on an apron she made: "Get thy spindle and distaff ready, and God will give thee flax".

Growing up in a household with civic-minded parents helped start Ethel on a life of public service. Mary Delafield Sturges, for example, started a project with the Kirkland Alumnae Association. There was talk that women workers in stores had no place to eat their lunches. Ethel's mother offered to fit up a room where the Association might

---

10   [15] File #17, the Dummer Collection, The Arthur & Elizabeth Schlesinger Library on the History of Women in America, 10 Garden Street, Cambridge, Massachusetts, hereafter referred to as the Dummer Collection

serve inexpensive lunches to these sales clerks as well as to other women. She recruited her daughter to help, seeing this as an activity for a young woman of her class who was not likely to be interested in a professional life. The lunch club grew and served its purpose for years. The Alumni Association also started an experiment at the Western Electric Factory serving lunch, dinner, and a midnight meal for men as well as women, a project later taken over by the factory. Ethel recalled later that she realized what her mother's wisdom had accomplished for her. She credits her mother as showing by example, opening new doors for her.

School was followed by a year of travel with an invalid brother. When his illness became active tuberculosis and her parents decided not to let Ethel spend the winter in Chicago, they permitted her and a younger sister to attend a boarding school near the home of Dr. D. Webster Prentiss, a family friend in Washington, D.C. While the school did not compare academically with the Kirkland School, Ethel's mental development continued, with a heavy reading load and evenings with teachers who came to her room to talk. "What a thrill I had", she states in her book, "when Dr. Prentiss invited me to go with him to the reception being given by the Cosmos Club for Alfred Wallace and I had a glimpse of the great evolutionist!" [8]

In 1887, Ethel's parents treated her to an educational trip to Alaska, another example of their education methods, which would be replicated in their daughter's priorities for her own family. In a three-page letter to her father from the *USS Manzanita*, she gives a detailed account of the trip north from Victoria Harbor, of gazing at snow-capped peaks along the Inland Passage and stopping to visit Indian villages along the Alaska coast. She tells of one day when she, her companion Annie, and a Mr. Seebree rowed to an out-of-the way Indian town that was having a special celebration and feast. Ethel and her companions were invited to attend the event, which she describes vividly in her letter. They visited another town, the poorest on the coast, of Flat Head Indians - so-called because they put boards on the heads of children so they would "develop rightly". One of Ethel's letters reveals what the trip meant to her:

"The days grow more delightful, the scenery is more grand and beautiful, and earth, sky and man seem to vie with each other in giving me joy. Mr. Seebree and Annie leave nothing undone for my pleasure; Mr. Hubbard sketches and is outlining a chart of our trip for me; the pilot tells me many things of interest about the country and the Indians; the first mate brings me glasses or telescope when the whales or porpoises appear; and the second mate gathers sea urchins and 'queer likes' for me to examine. Father dear, I thank you from my heart for all this happiness which you have given me. 'It is more blessed to give than to receive.' I have the happiness, you are blessed." [11][17]

Marriage and the Young Dummer Family

A major change in her life awaited Ethel when she returned from her Alaska trip. Her father had given the position of bank vice-president to his legal advisor on financial matters, William Francis Dummer, known as Frank. Dummer, born in 1851, was the son of Judge Henry Enoch and Phoebe Dummer of Jacksonville, Illinois. Judge Dummer was a friend and colleague of Abraham Lincoln before he became President. (Numerous letters to "Friend Dummer" are now in the Lincoln Library at Springfield, Illinois.) Like the Sturges family, Dummer's ancestors had emigrated from England to New England, in this case to Massachusetts, in the 17th century. At seventeen, observing his father's failing health, Frank Dummer gave up college, studied law and was admitted to the bar while clerking in a Bloomingdale bank. He passed the bar exam without having attended law school.

During a long illness of one of their sons, George and Mary Delafield Sturges came to depend on Frank Dummer. He became a friend of the whole family, young and old. Ethel describes developing a strong friendship with this "older man" fifteen years her senior. When her engagement to Frank was announced, a Sturges friend asked if it had been a long engagement. "Yes", Ethel's mother replied, "but the two of them were almost the last to discover it." Even before marriage, Ethel commented years later, she and Frank Dummer planned a home that

---

[11] 8 Dummer Book, pp. 14-17
[17] #18, Dummer Collection

would draw into it all possible values from outside, and pour into the lives of others the best they could provide. She describes the developing relationship they both became aware of before marriage as a "telepathic transfer" indicating "a rare type of attraction or sympathy. Throughout forty years together", Ethel relates, her husband's "quiet spiritual nature radiated to us all strength and courage and a great peace. This indicates a picture which is quite beyond words to express." [12][18]

Ethel and Frank were married at Snug Harbor in Lake Geneva in 1888. The ceremony was attended by over 100 people, mostly from Chicago, but also including relatives from the large Sturges clan who now had second homes in Lake Geneva. After a honeymoon in Florida, the newlyweds moved into a home built on the site of the Solomon Sturges house, Ethel's birthplace that had been destroyed in the fire. The new, four-story house was across the street from the George Sturges house where Ethel lived until her marriage.

Ethel thought about and expressed their intimate relationship at a time when this was infrequently discussed within their strata of society. "That Mr. Dummer was one of ten children and I one of nine, may have made for our successful mating. I believe statisticians count it of value." They "took life simply, meeting the joys and sorrows, our own and those of others, with faith in what might be. When, later, science forced people to bring up into consciousness the physical side of sex, I often thought to myself that this ancient part of our system would function better and more naturally if the conscious mind were not so focused upon it; that it was like the digestive process which worked well when left without worry of our intellectual concern."[13] The Dummers were soon blessed with four daughters: Marion, born in 1890; Katharine in 1892; Ethel (later nicknamed Happy) in 1895; and Frances, born in 1899. A son born after the girls did not survive to his first birthday.

Frank Dummer had a theory about how children learn. At age fourteen he had visited the Illinois State Institution for the deaf and dumb and watched methods of teaching deaf-mutes to speak. If this method can

---

12   [18] Dummer Book, p. 20
13   Dummer Book, pp. 28

accomplish so much with such handicapped children, he reasoned, what might it do for normal children? When his four daughters were very young he began testing his theory. During baby Marion's first year, as she started to move around and explore, her father began to teach her to make every sound in English before she was a year old. Beginning by imitating a sound she made, he repeated it. This seemed to establish a certain rapport, after which it was a type of play, Marion imitating her father's sounds or possibly the shape of his mouth as he formed them. He was always careful to limit such play, stopping short of inattention or fatigue. Ethel soon realized that her husband had a deeper psychological understanding of child development than she had. [14]

Frank Dummer also believed that the most important factor in educating little children was coordination of sense and muscle; everything that increased muscle coordination had great value. When each daughter attempted her first step he did not reach out to help, instinctively believing that the baby's brain would better retain the motor task and accomplishment if she did not rely on an adult's help. (His theory would be verified by neurologists and educators with the help of new technology almost a century later.) He invented finger games to help teach control and finger arithmetic to give a sense of number combinations. Creeping, climbing, and later swinging, riding a bicycle, and especially swimming were encouraged. As they grew, their father also taught them how to find out what they wanted to know in the dictionary and encyclopedia. As control of the body gave self-reliance and confidence, both parents believed, so did the ability to rely upon their own minds.

In her autobiography, completed in 1935, Ethel Dummer refers to two instances where her husband's theories were similar to and may have influenced some pioneering educators. When he talked to Mrs. Helen Woolley about her nursery school at Michigan's Merrill Palmer Training School, he told her she began teaching young children too late. The most important year for learning, he believed, was before a child's eighteenth month. In another reference Ethel Dummer notes that years later the Dummers met Dr. and Mrs. Arnold Gesell of the Yale Laboratory at a Child Welfare Conference in Los Angeles. The

14 Dummer Book, pp. 22-23

Gesells were surprised to learn that Frank Dummer had carried on observations and experiments with his children, somewhat similar to theirs, years before the Yale Laboratory was established.[15]

Metamorphosis 1900-1920

Ethel had reached adulthood during what has come to be called the "Progressive Era", about 1890-1920, when men and women of honorable spirit were increasingly engaged on social and civic problems. Her upbringing prepared her for emerging as what came later to be called a "community housekeeper". The term refers to the belief that some women of her time, accustomed to organizing their home environments to ensure their family's well being, were also interested in working to improve the moral and social order of their surroundings. Religious values, particularly of the white Protestant majority in which Ethel had been exposed, encouraged a sense of maternalism. Women were urged to improve individual and cultural regeneration through volunteerism and other good works. Teachers at the Kirkland School, who emphasized the social service obligations of wealthy women, influenced Ethel during her formative years. [16]

Both men and women were questioning how democratic and religious institutions and values could survive the strains of the Industrial Revolution with its increasing emphasis on the marketplace. The publication of Darwin's *Origin of Species* in 1859, for example, challenged the moral and ethical obligations of Judeo-Christian traditions. Historian Kathryn Kish Sklar uses the term "moral materialism" to describe the late 19th century period when the materialism of the post-Darwin world combined with those from an earlier era with implications for civic-minded adults. [17]

By far the most important influence on developing young Ethel's interest in community service was the example set by her mother. At the end of the century Mary Delafield Sturges was becoming interested

---

15   Dummer Book, pp. 20-25
16   *Notable American women - the Modern Period* ; p. 208
17   *Florence Kelley &Tthe Nation's Work* by Kathryn Kish Sklar, Yale University, 1995; p. *xii*

in supporting a group called the Juvenile Protective Association (JPA), in which her daughter would soon become heavily involved. In 1889 some members of the Chicago Women's Club had been concerned that the same court that handled criminals dispensed decisions relating to hapless children. Interested in improving conditions for children in police stations and jails, they formed the JPA and drafted a bill proposing a Juvenile Court. After nine years of hard work, the Illinois State Legislature passed a Juvenile Court Law. The Chicago Juvenile Court, the first in the world and an example for many others, opened in 1899. The law did not appropriate funds for the Court's administration. Ethel learned later that her mother provided funds for the first probation officer.

Chicago was setting an example for social reform in other ways. In 1889 Jane Addams had opened the Hull House Settlement to serve the city's immigrant community. (The term "settlement" was used for community centers in poor neighborhoods.) Hull House would soon become a model for urban reform in major American cities; Addams would become a national and international voice for the rights of the poor, particularly women and children. After a happy childhood in a small country town, this daughter of a state senator had come to believe that one of the greatest things wrong with society was a neglect and misunderstanding of what youth needed to progress to adulthood.[18] She had dropped out of medical school due to illness, then toured Europe with her friend Ellen Gates Starr, who had been one of Dummer's teachers at the Kirkland School. On her return she decided to devote her life to helping the needy in a city slum.

Addams was also looking for a way for unmarried, educated women to become socially useful in respectable ways.[19] She wanted to persuade them to help in civic service rather than pursuing the "endless, profitless round of pleasure-seeking" that was their usual lot. There was no school of social work at the time to prepare people for what was to become a profession.

---

18   *Jane Addams - Pioneer for Social Justice,* by Cornelia Meigs, Little Brown & Co. Boston, 1970
19   *Fifty Years of Pioneering,* File #406, Dummer Collection

Chicago had become a major shipping center for grain, cattle, and lumber, as well as a large manufacturing city. Ruthless businessmen who headed some of the major companies had little consideration for working conditions and wages. Large numbers of immigrants had come to the city from Europe, Ireland, Germany and Russia, eager for jobs, ignorant of the cost of living and the unendurable conditions for workers. There were plenty of needy people in Chicago's slums when Jane Addams and Ellen Starr co-founded Hull House. To launch their new endeavor, they found a large house in a setting perfect for them. It was in an immigrant neighborhood with muddy, garbage-strewn streets, where children played in narrow alleys and people talked many languages.[20] The initial purpose of the settlement was to meet basic needs in the neighborhood. The women started with a nursery and progressed to teaching the children of working mothers; they soon began to investigate ways to improve general living conditions. Ethel Sturges Dummer would soon become a Hull House trustee, directly involved in many of the settlement's activities. Her role of community housekeeper was launched. By 1920 it would expand throughout Chicago, to Southern California and beyond.

To appreciate the contrast of Ethel's upbringing to activities in which she was about to embark it is helpful to know a little more about her family background. Solomon Sturges, her paternal grandfather, was a very wealthy man, as were members of his large, extended family. Sturges, whose forebears had immigrated to New England from England in 1623, was born in 1796 in Fairfield, Connecticut. At age nineteen he moved to Putnam, Ohio (which later became Zanesfield), where he quickly moved up from clerk to partner in his brother-in-law Ebinezer Buckingham's store. In 1823 he married Lucy Hale from Connecticut who, a book about him and his family reports, had a magnetic influence on his life. [21]

The business interests of the large Buckingham and Sturges families grew rapidly and prospered. Sturges soon had extensive land holdings in Illinois and nearby states. He foresaw a rich future for the region, with Chicago as a grain distribution center for the country and a hungry

---

20   Jane Addams, by Gail Faithful Keller, Crowell Biography, 1971
21   *Solomon Sturges Memoir,* pp. 29 & 31

world. One of his sons and a partner founded a company that built the first grain elevator in Chicago, a venture Solomon Sturges joined in 1855. When the canal project to connect Toledo with Evansville on the Ohio River fell behind schedule, Sturges and three partners contracted to finish the project. When it was finally completed, the partners shared a profit of $80,000, a large sum at the time.

In 1855 Sturges moved his family to Chicago. He negotiated an agreement with the Illinois Central Railroad to build and operate a grain warehouse, which came to store nearly a quarter of the grain passing through the city. To help convince his wife of the move from their comfortable home to the boom-town of Chicago, he purchased half of a block by Pine and Huron Streets and built what was then considered one of the finest dwellings in the city – but she died before it was finished. Over the years Sturges expanded his interests to include ownership of grain-carrying vessels on the Great Lakes and proprietorship of a fleet of tugboats in Chicago Harbor. With three of his sons, he established the banking firm of Sturges and Sons, with his son William as manager. [22] Though her grandfather died two years before Ethel Sturges was born, he had built a family fortune and position into which she was born and raised.

Coming from a home world of bright, refined friends in a city and country life that included interests in travel and the joy of children, Ethel had little conception of the lives of most of humanity. In her autobiography she describes an event that had a profound effect on her life. One summer morning, about 1905, she was stunned by an advertisement of the National Child Labor Committee, with facts and pictures, which asked, "Do you know that thousands of children work through a ten-hour day or a ten-hour night?" She asked her husband if this was possible. It had never been brought to his attention, he replied. When a small contribution brought the Dummers all of the Committee's literature, a social conscience was born. From a trim and orderly garden, Ethel later recalled, she slipped into a jungle. Surely in my generation, she thought, there must be many others "blinded by the sunshine of their lives to the shadows in others". Together with Jane Addams, the Dummers attended the National Conference on Child

22 Dummer Book, pp. 37-40

Labor in Cincinnati the following autumn. From that time on, there was friendly betting among the young Dummer daughters as to how many minutes would pass before their mother injected the subject of her new interest into the conversation. [23]

Another incident the same year also influenced Ethel Dummer. She had read or heard a statement that no mother was the right type of mother for all ages of her children. She believed that she had done a good job of mothering her children during their early years, but as her daughters reached puberty, she felt a need to expand her interests and develop a new relationship with them. Her metamorphosis to a new role began. The game of humanity, she wrote a friend later, became more enthralling than was a game of golf to her friends.[24] The Dummer library began to reflect these changes in focus of the household. From well-bound editions of poets, essayists, historians, and biography, a corner developed which her daughters called "Mother's shelves". These included books and articles on sociology, psychology and biology, and journals of social hygiene (the term mental health came later), criminology, labor legislation and the International Journal of Ethics. [25]

During the Progressive Era women were beginning to offer an effective alternative to the male- dominated status quo. Kathryn Kish Sklar uses the term "public culture" to describe how women influenced the distribution of social resources, how they participated in public affairs, and how they built institutions to facilitate their participation. Their involvement took many forms, including the protection of women and children in the workplace as well as in the home.[26]

Ethel Sturges Dummer sometimes referred to herself as a feminist. She referred to that term in her graduation speech; it also heads one of the chapters in her autobiography. Was she a feminist? Webster's Dictionary defines feminism as "(1) the theory of the political, economic and social equality of the sexes, and (2) organized activity on behalf of women's rights and interests". In her book *The Grounding*

---

23   Dummer Book, pp. 33-34
24   #230, Dummer Collection
25   Dummer Book, p. 34
26   Ibid. pp. *xi & xiii*

of Modern Feminism women's historian Nancy F. Cott states that the word feminist is not tied to a specific time in history. Over time it has had different meanings to different people. Cott defines feminism as having three inexact components: the belief in sexual equality, the belief that women's condition is shaped by human social usage rather than predestined by God or nature, and that women see themselves as having a group identity. What had been referred to in the nineteenth-century as the "woman movement", by the 1910s transferred into various avenues of social, economic, and political power from which women felt excluded. By 1913 the word feminism was being used frequently, but there was no common definition of the term.

Many people today looking back on the women's role at the turn of the century may think first of applying the term feminist largely to women fighting for their rights, most prominently the right to vote. They were outspoken and visible. Dummer was clearly not marching in the streets. She once told a publisher she did not want to have her name on anything that would seem to be a craving for publicity. She was, however, an active and vocal advocate of women and children's rights, of social and legal reform of conditions related to marriage, inheritance and penal laws.

Financial assistance was a largely "invisible" way Ethel helped the reform movement. In most cases she did not want her financial backing mentioned. In a letter sending her the Juvenile Court's 1916 report, Chief Probation Officer Joel D. Hunter thanked her, on behalf of the officers and employees, for her assistance in signing the indemnity bond for the Court's operation. Mentioning the benefits to the welfare of many children over the first four years, he ended with the note, "You deserve a great deal more thanks than anyone else." [27]

The Juvenile Protective Association (JPA) was incorporated in 1907 with Mrs. Louise deKoven Bowen as President. [28] Due to its convenient location opposite the Juvenile Court, the new organization was housed at Hull House. The women who ran Hull House were becoming aware of Ethel Dummer's new interest in child labor issues. In 1905 she was

---

27 #373, Dummer Collection
28 *Notable American Women*, p. 100

invited to join the JPA and to serve on its board. In addition to the treatment of children in Juvenile Court, the JPA women were concerned that homeless and orphaned children were placed in institutions. They also questioned having children over ten years old designated as "delinquents" (a general Progressive Era term that encompassed a wide range of young transgressors) and sent to police stations, the Criminal Court, and prison. Judge Pinkney of the Juvenile Court, who shared some of their concerns, urged them to continue their research on the causes of delinquency in children and efforts toward its prevention.

Ethel soon became a key member of this effort, and it became an important transition to a new phase of her life. "Many a time when the day came which brought this difficult duty, I struggled against a sensation almost of nausea, as I knew the time had come again to listen to stories of lives so sordid and indecent. One day as I returned through those slum streets toward the trolley, suddenly I saw that only by being willing to take into our minds and hearts the knowledge of the world as it is can we help make it what it should be. Never having been able to find vicarious suffering reasonable, I then saw that this was what Jane Addams and Mary McDowell (head resident at the University of Chicago Settlement) were living -- that unless we took into our consciousness the sins and sufferings of humanity we could not solve them." [29]

Because of her success in helping to raise money for a detention home, Judge Pinkney appointed Dummer to the JPA's Research Committee on Delinquency - It's Causes and Prevention.

The first year of JPA Committee work shocked her, as case after case taught her the realities of life. She would return to her husband saying, "any one of the cases reported today would break the heart, but when thirty are heard, it hits the brain". Common sense told her the children were not to blame, that adults should see to it that the environment was improved. Prevention, she came to believe, is better than cure. During her weekly visits to Hull House and its neighborhood, she was awakening to the realities of families she visited living in the "jungle" of Chicago's poorer area, compared to the "garden" of her life as wife,

29   Dummer Book, pp 34-35

mother, and link with members of the large Sturges and Dummer clans.

Asked to look at individual cases, she went each Friday morning to listen to the case reports. "Their stories were so depressing, so sordid, with the squalor and degeneracy of those drab slum lives, that only duty, that stern goddess, drove me to the West Side." [30] The experience led Ethel to believe that children sent to the Juvenile Court were not bad, but needed interesting activities. The right kind of education, she thought, would prevent much truant and delinquent behavior. The research department of the Chicago School of Civics and Philanthropy, of which Dummer was a founding trustee, was reporting that a large proportion of "feeblemindedness" (a general term used at the time) was not noticeable in very young children. Dummer claimed that ninety-five percent of these delinquents would be good children in the right environment, that only a few who repeated delinquent behavior were doubtful. She believed that these children with abnormal behavior needed the counseling of a wise physician. For example, at a meeting at Hull House one morning, a number of cases of incest were reported. They included a case of one man who upon the death of his wife, had, before the funeral, taken his little daughter to his bed. This seemed to her to need explanation rather then condemnation of the girl. She emphasized that a doctor rather than a judge could help them understand the case.

Ethel Dummer began to develop the idea of a psychological clinic for Juvenile Court children. The effort initially fell on deaf ears; for several years JPA members and others were not receptive. "I still recall the torrent of legal phraseology poured out upon me by a judge when I suggested that a wise physician rather than a man trained in law would be of value in the Juvenile Court", Dummer writes. [31] Finally, however, Dummer helped persuade committee members that a more scientific approach to analyzing causes was a necessary step to preventing delinquent behavior. Together they inquired, but could find no evidence of, a scientific study of the mind of the juvenile delinquent to

---

30   Ibid. p. 45 - 46
31   Dummer Book, p. 50

help them distinguish early the types of children they thought should be segregated.

As Ethel wrestled with these problems her attention was caught by a small book by Mary Everest Boole, mistakenly put in her mailbox, titled *The Preparation of the Child for Science.* The accidental discovery would have a profound effect on her life and her interests. Mrs. Boole's deceased husband, George Boole, had been a prominent British mathematician and logician. He had taught that no conclusion was valid that conflicted with one's belief and position until all phases of a problem had been studied. This book, including Mary Boole's interpretation of her husband's *Laws of Thought*, illuminated for Dummer the kind of problems she had been pondering. The new information underscored Dummer's conviction that withholding condemnation until all facts are obtained was logical, that she was following the right path before forming her opinion about a solution to a problem. The Booles' logic revealed for her what real thinking involved. It was later clarified for her in a hypothesis of Dr. William White, an administrator at the Institute of Child Guidance in New York: "Through solution of conflict, higher levels of mental integration are attained." While conflict resolution is a fairly common part of problem-solving strategy today, these ideas were a revelation to Ethel Dummer and many others at the beginning of the 20th century. She traced an idea she was developing for a juvenile clinic to the thoughts of Mary Everest Boole and to Valery- Radot's *Life of Pasteur*, which she read in 1907.

Mrs. Boole had written that progress occurs in crises. A crisis takes place when the science making the most advancement turns its attention to the class of humanity most in need. Boole had prophesied twenty-five years earlier that the next great step would be taken when psychology studied the criminal and the insane. Dummer compared this to her reading about Pasteur, how he had discovered and controlled the germs that were eventually killing plants, animals and at last man. The thought flashed into her mind: "In some psychological laboratory there must even now be at work the man who shall prevent much crime and insanity". On inquiring, she found that nowhere in the world was the typical delinquent child being specifically studied. [32]

32 Dummer Book, pp. 47-53

Armed with new ideas about how to resolve conflicts in crisis situations, Ethel Dummer invited to her home a small group of scientists and philanthropists to discuss cases of children who became truant or delinquent without apparent reason. The concept was further discussed at a second meeting at Hull House called by the JPA. Dummer was being further drawn in to the group of women working to improve support services for children. They included Hull House resident physician Alice Hamilton and another resident, Jessie Florence Binford. The latter was an investigator for the Legal Aid Society who had fought for and won a division of policewomen specifically trained to handle juvenile cases. Binford later became superintendent of the JPA.

In 1909 the women's efforts were rewarded by the creation of the world's first child guidance clinic, chartered by the State of Illinois as the Juvenile Psychopathic Institute. Julia Lathrop, another Hull House resident, became chair of the new organization's board. Created to support the work of the Juvenile Court and the JPA, it was initially called the Psychopathic Clinic for the Study of Delinquent Children. The name was later changed to The Institute for Juvenile Research (IJR), which it is still called. Dummer later described her role in the IJR's beginning: as a JPA board member, she came to realize that most children sent to the Juvenile Court were not bad, but needed interesting activities. She believed that the right kind of education would prevent aberrant behavior, that it was when life was not worthwhile that these children became truant and delinquent There were certain children, however, who "without rhyme or reason repeated some one symptom of delinquency, either stealing, lying or sex offenses. These were so abnormal that I urged scientific research concerning the causes."

At the suggestion of Julia Lathrop, distinguished psychiatrist Dr. William Healy, already successful with handling atypical children, was recruited to head the new Institute. Ethel Dummer is credited as chiefly responsible for securing his services. [33] "At the time", Dr. Healy later reported, "there was not even a semblance of anything that could be called a well-rounded study of a young human individual. Psychological norms were not available, standardized mental tests had

---

33   From *The Proceedings of The Institute of Medicine of Chicago*, Nov. 15, 1954, Vol. 20, #8

to be developed; ...the importance of knowledge of family attitude and conditioning was barely realized." [34] Dummer offered Judge Pinkney the services of Dr. Healy and his staff. With assistance from her sisters, Ethel Dummer underwrote the cost of the new organization's operation for the first five years. [35]

Dummer describes one of Dr. Healy's cases that she believed particularly revealed a possible cause of delinquency. A young Italian immigrant girl who showed no mental difficulty and was bright in her lessons suddenly began to steal, without any apparent reason. When Dr. Healy asked her what she thought about just before she took something, she answered "The name of John. If I see it in my reading lessons I have to take something." Children seemed to pour out to Dr. Healy what was troubling them. The girl told him about a little boy who had made indecent suggestions to her. She had resisted, but had gone with him while they took some fruit from the corner grocery. Whenever the experience came to her mind, she found an outlet in stealing. The interesting thing about the case was that from the moment she told this to Dr. Healy, the stealing ceased. When Dummer described the case and was asked "why", she could not answer. "What causes behavior?" she pondered. This and similar cases prepared her to read and understand the work of Freud, and later of Pavlov of conditioning reflexes as motivation below the conscious level. [36]

When she told a friend, the wife of a university professor, about how much Healy was doing for misunderstood children, the friend replied: "Well, if what you want is to help a few children that is one thing, but as for his work being scientific, it simply isn't." She was not the only skeptic. Other critics did not see the value in Healy's work. Because the Clinic was privately funded, some raised questions about whether the case histories Healy was compiling belonged to him or to Cook County. Alarmed that his files might be turned over to the Civil Service, Healy

---

34 *Twenty-Five Years of Child Guidance,* by William Healy, Dept. of Public Welfare, Illinois; Series C. No. 256. Studies for Juvenile Research, p. 2
35 #242; Dummer Collection; *Women Building Chicago ...(etc.)*; p. 82
36 Dummer Book, pp. 50-53

told Ethel Dummer he was glad the Clinic's records were safely stored in Mr. Dummer's vault at the bank. [37]

Contrary to some negative assessments, Healy was successful in introducing his philosophy of a multidisciplinary, team approach to the study and treatment of behavior disorders in children. His work began to be recognized and accepted with publication of his first book, *The Individual Delinquent*. It quickly sold over a thousand copies, and was used at Northwestern University's

Law School. The new clinic was visited by people from near and far. When Healy lectured at the Harvard Summer School in 1912, social workers "were thrilled at his interpretation of the causes of behavior both delinquent and neurotic." In *Mental Conflict and Misconduct*, Dr. Healy analyzed the causes of behavior showing the influence of emotion on "ideation-behavior", and how unburdening conscious and unconscious troubles could set children free. The expression "ideation-behavior" registered deeply in Ethel's mind. She continued to further ponder the causes of so-called feeblemindedness and delinquent behavior in children, and on the nature of the thinking process.

In 1914, when Haley and his wife Dr. Augusta Bronner moved on to head the Judge Baker Guidance Center in Boston, Cook County assumed financial support of the Chicago clinic as an adjunct of the Juvenile Court. The State of Illinois accepted responsibility for its operation in 1917. State Criminologist Herman Adler became director when the State made it part of the Department of Public Welfare. Thus began a dynamic new era of court psychiatry. Rosco Pond, for many years Dean of the Harvard Law School, called establishment of the Institute for Juvenile Research the greatest advance in judicial procedure since the Magna Carta. [38] On the IJR's fiftieth anniversary in February 1960, Superintendent Raymond E. Robertson, M.D. honored Ethel Dummer, calling her a generous and enlightened civic leader, and an ardent student of newly emerging theories of the unconscious, as more than any other person responsible for the beginning and early years of the Institute. [39]

37 #578, 7/26/11, Dummer Collection
38 The Welfare Bulletin, Illinois Department of Public Welfare, Nov./Dec. 1952
39 Family records.

We can only guess at the sense of satisfaction Ethel Sturges Dummer must have felt as she began to see results of her part in the new role she was creating: a combination catalyst, joint problem-solver and philanthropist. Her long relationship with Dr. Haley would last until her death in 1954.

While much of her attention was focused on the IJR, Dummer kept in touch with what was happening at the Juvenile Court. She reported to a friend that Judge Pinkney had appointed attorney Mary Bartelme, a social feminist and juvenile reformer, assistant judge to hear girls' cases at the Court. Bartelme was one of the founders of the Chicago Business Woman's Club, created to support women professionals. She had been the first woman Public Guardian of Cook County, involved in the campaign to establish a Juvenile Court. She had also worked with other women reformers to found a detention home as an alternative to jail for juvenile girls who came before the new Court. Bartelme tried placing girls in homes instead of institutions. In four months, Dummer reported, only three girls out of ninety-seven were returned to the court. At every opportunity Ethel Dummer commended the progress being shown by Chicago judges connected to the Juvenile Court.[40]

Civic Affairs

There were profound differences at the turn of the century between men's and women's concepts about how city government should address urban problems. Members of Chicago's all-male City Club (of which Frank Dummer was a founding member) were primarily interested in efficiency and the good of the business community. Women were more interested in health, welfare and the comfort of all citizens. Women went out into the streets to investigate, while men relied on employees to gather facts and figures. Much of the women's activity was carried out through women's clubs. Louise DeKoven Bowen, president of the Women's City Club formed in 1910, expressed an optimistic question in a speech. "Suppose we had a system of municipal relief which is built

---

40 #230, Dummer Collection; and *Notable American Women* ...; p. 60/61; *Women Building Chicago* ..., p. 67

on the principle that the community is one great family and that each member of it is bound to help the other, the burden of support falling on all alike?" [41] One has to wonder if she thought this ideal was even remotely possible.

In 1894-95 Jane Addams had organized women to go out and clean the streets themselves when the city was doing little about the problem. The all-male City Club favored private operation of services such as garbage collection, with limited municipal power. "In designing solutions to problems, they made fiscal efficiency and financial profitability the criteria for evaluating proposals for change." [42] Members of the Women's City Club had other priorities. They used the term "municipal housekeeping". [43] The Club expanded rapidly until it represented thirty separate women's organizations. The membership included both professional and non-professional women, a distinction not clearly drawn at that time. A number of members were wives of members of the (men's) City Club. The women stressed health and welfare over economic needs, and they believed that municipal control would make for a healthier environment. To pursue their interests, the Club directed member Mary McDowell of the University of Chicago Settlement to explore the various sanitation methods of other major cities in the United States and Europe. Ethel Sturges Dummer financed McDowell's travels, another example of her emerging philanthropic style. [44]

Upon her return, McDowell put together a coalition of supporters, drawn from men's and women's clubs and University of Chicago faculty, to demand improvements of Chicago's sanitation. In this instance men's and women's groups acted together; the combined influential group brought results. Mayor Carter Harrison appointed a City Waste Commission, of which McDowell was a member, and promised to

---

41   *Gender and Urban Political Reform: The City Club and the Women's City Club of Chicago in the Progressive Era*, Maureen A. Flanagan, AHA Journal
42   Ibid. pp 1044
43   *Women Building Chicago ... ".* p. 1048
44   "Gender and Urban Political Reform: The City Club and the Women's City Club of Chicago in the Progressive Era" by Maureen A. Flanagan ; AHA Journal; *Women Building Chicago ...*; p. 564

fund engineers to devise solutions to the city's waste problems. Chicago followed the commission's recommendations. Noxious open dumps where children had played were gradually phased out.

The Dummers' approach was not typical of differing views between the sexes about how to solve social problems. The McDowell trip and its outcome provides an example of a shared interest. They were evolving a partnership based on like-minded interests and ideas about problem solving; they both credited Mary McDowell with greatly influencing their point of view. McDowell had given Frank Dummer Frederick Howe's *The City, the Hope of Democracy*, and she had drawn Ethel into the work of the University of Chicago Settlement, on which the latter served as a trustee. (In 1916 McDowell, who became a good friend of Ethel's, influenced the directors of the Women's City Club to create a new department of education.) [45] In monthly dinner meetings of the Settlement's Board of Directors, discussions were expected, and included spouses. One evening they heard a report on malnutrition and diseases found in the children who attended two public schools in the stockyard neighborhood. Miss McDowell commented that no family could live according to decent American standards on the laborer's wages. The Settlement Board engaged Professor John C. Kennedy of the University of Chicago's Economics Department to survey the situation.

About this time, Ethel was trying to locate a boy who was demoralizing several groups, investigating to report the case at a JPA meeting. [46] She came upon Miss A. B. Reynolds, a big-hearted, broad-minded principal who knew the background of boys and girls in her school. She was making a real difference, helping to gain support of families in the surrounding slum neighborhood. Reynolds was offering her services free for the summer if the Board of Education would keep the school open for recreation during the afternoon. The experience was so successful that Dummer and Reynolds signed a petition to use the Kinzie School two evenings a week the following winter. Illustrated lectures were offered for adults; a library, story telling and games for

45   #650, Dummer Collection
46   Dummer Book, pp 35-37

young people; singing, gymnastics and dancing were offered for all. In an attempt to brighten the lives of children and families in the Kinzie school area, Ethel hired a folk dance instructor to add to activities at the center's evening programs. She also helped at the center one evening a week. Her heart was touched one evening when a dark-eyed mother with a black shawl over her head came up to her and said, through a friend who interpreted, that she had danced the same dances in the old country.

The weekly experiences at the center convinced Ethel that supplying the right kind of wholesome activities together with some food would be successful for a majority of children in the slum neighborhoods and perhaps in others areas. She compared her new experiences learning "how the other half lived" with activities in the Dummer home. She came to believe in the value of these kinds of activities generally for home-school relationships, as well as for the marriage relationship in the children's homes. Situations in slum homes set her to thinking about the particular problems of unmarried mothers, which led to a desire to expand her knowledge of human relationships generally.

Ethel's knowledge of the city continued to grow, as did her determination to help solve its problems. Her associations with like-minded people expanded. These experiences in slum areas helped turn her mind to civics as an avenue to attack problems. Through her interest in the mental hygiene work of Julia Lathrop, who had established an experiment in therapy through hard work in Dummer's neighborhood, Ethel was attracted to The Chicago School of Civics and Philanthropy (CSCP), first created to train those who provided social services, officially chartered in 1908. (It would later become the University of Chicago's School of Social Service Administration, expanding to include more scientific investigation and to act as a clearing-house of information for social and civic workers in towns and cities of the midwest. At that time the University of Chicago was a national leader in the field of sociology.) Professor Graham Taylor of the Sociology Department served as president of the CSCP, Julia Lathrop as vice president and director of research, and Ethel Dummer agreed to become secretary. The Board also included Jane Addams, Anita McCormick Blaine and Louise DeKoven Bowen. Edward L. Burchard was the Director of the Extension Department that disseminated information. A Handbook of City Welfare Aids and Opportunities was an early example of the organization's outreach activities. It was distributed throughout the city to civic organizations, churches, schools, and libraries with the financial aid of Ethel's youngest sister, Clara Sturges Johnson. The publication listed sources of aid, exhibits, a lecture series, film and slide show information, as well as literature included in the school's library. [47]

About this time Frank Dummer brought home the book *All the Children of All the People* by Illinois educator William Hawley Smith. It added to the Dummers' sense of responsibility for public school children. Their interests became centered on science and education, their work on various civic committees connected with public schools. One of Frank Dummer's special interests was of foreign nationals grouping together like small cities within growing municipalities. In 1911 he went to Europe with the Boston Chamber of Commerce for a tour of civic governments there. [48] His hobby was maps, so he had detailed real estate maps of Chicago. The Dummers devised a way to pinpoint on maps and charts the "disreputable districts" that were demoralizing children. They gave the maps to the JPA office, where they were copied for distribution to other organizations. The Dummers mounted a plan for their own district on a breadboard. They used colored pins to mark locations of places they believed were having positive and negative impact on children. Black pins showed saloons and pool rooms, white showed churches, and gold pins showed the two settlements. They then invited clergymen, school principals and some neighbors to their home for an evening to hear Mrs. W. Thomas of the JPA describe situations they were uncovering which were contributing to delinquency. Miss Reynolds was also there and, according to her hostess, made quite an impression. At the end of the evening the Dummers' philanthropic friends asked "What do you want us to do?" "To know, to become aware of the situation." Ethel answered.[49]

---

47 #299, Dummer Collection
48 #219, Dummer Collection
49 Dummer Book, pp. 37-38

The plan for the CSCP's first "Social Museum Exhibit" in 1910 showed the framework and functions of an ideal town. These were illustrated in nine sections, with the best pictorial examples from various cities on subjects such as city organization, public safety, charities, corrections, education and recreation. Planners hoped it would eventually be used as a traveling exhibit to cities within a 100-mile radius of Chicago, and to midwestern universities, thus advertising the work of the School.

In 1912 the CSCP presented a three-day City Welfare Exhibit of maps, charts, posters and pictures with explanatory texts and figures showing conditions and suggesting improvements in various matters of public health, public utilities and public service. It incorporated suggestions by both Dummers. Offered through the auspices of the Women's Club in cooperation with park and public school authorities, it was designed to enlighten and inform citizens about Chicago at that time, and to raise hopes and excite ambitions to make the City what it ought to be. The day and evening programs also included everything from a reception, singing and "gymnastic dancing" by students, to a physician's demonstration on the care of a baby. Extension Department director Edward L. Burchard later questioned the fruitfulness of using graphs showing relative numbers and proportions. Some people in their audiences seemed confused by so many facts and figures; he believed the information would not be remembered. It would be interesting to ask the "common man" and school children for their reactions, he tactfully wrote Dummer. [50] A member of the Chicago School Board wrote ESD attesting to the benefits of the Civic Exhibits given throughout the city. He believed they were leaving a lasting impression on the minds of children and gave food for thought to Parent Teacher Association members. A few days after Miss McDowell compared the garbage handling in other cities, he told her, a garbage wagon was nearly mobbed by the children because there was no cover on the wagon. [51]

Ethel refers to the Dummers' civic involvement at this time as "quite a three-ring circus". As a director of the CSCP and chairman of a Women's City Club committee, Ethel had the responsibility to take

---

50   #300, #301 & #306, Dummer Collection
51   Dummer Collection

the Child Welfare Exhibit to public schools and field houses in small parks. Her daughters, then ages 12-22, called her Mrs. Pooh Bah. She "commandeered" (her word) Mr. Burchard to prepare the civic exhibit to give publicity not only to the human needs learned in school and settlement work, but also to European experiments in bettering similar situations. The exhibit was explained to eighth grade students, who were asked to interpret it to their parents. The following summer, at Frank Dummer's request (and probably with the Dummers' financial support), Burchard went abroad to collect material on how municipal affairs being conducted in foreign cities might suggest improving methods in America. When he returned he made displays on "What the Old World Has to Teach the New", which were included in the exhibits sent to the schools. [52]

The Dummer Family

While Ethel and Frank Dummer were becoming civil servants, they were certainly not neglecting the joys and responsibilities of parenthood. Although they had a nurse for the girls when they were young, Ethel took charge of their physical needs and read to them a great deal. Because the parents believed that schools of that period hampered mental development, the girls were educated at home during early years by carefully selected teachers. They were fortunate to secure teachers who were advanced relative to the norms of the day. One wall of the playroom in the Dummer home was finished in green to be used as a chalk board. On it the girls began writing with free strokes, using their arms instead of their wrists and fingers. Frank Dummer objected to the use of small muscles, insisting that large muscles should be used first, when children were younger. Their teacher, Miss Menefee, gave the children Norse and Greek myths, which they expressed in some art form, clay, painting or drama. The girls also used the chalk board for beginning writing and academic subjects.

Another feature the Dummers introduced was in the top floor of the Dummer home: a large closet known as the Glory Hole. It contained clothing and costumes used for fancy dress affairs and home dramatics,

---

52   #230, Dummer Collection, Dummer Book, p. 42

materials, and silver. Nearby was an old chiffonier called Chaos, with drawers filled with tools, a wood-carving set, paints, crayons and odds and ends. "Many an idea was worked out up there and many a mood worked off. Constructive activity is a great safety-valve", Dummer wrote in her autobiography.

The children also spent a great deal of time outdoors. Their parents had agreed that when one of them started an activity with a child, the other was to show no fear. Ethel often went into the house when she saw the children's risky activities, such as an 8-year-old daughter swinging on a trapeze without using her hands.

The Dummers built a summer home they called the Orchard on a hill above Lake Geneva. Half of the 40 acres was woods; the other half included a farm, a barn, fruit trees, and a field for making hay for the horses. One year they engaged a Scotch carpenter and let the girls help him build a two-story playhouse, used for many years by their children and later by grandchildren.

Ethel, who had always had a hankering to use tools, pitched in. She helped saw the sideboards and work on window casings. When she saw her children up on top helping to shingle the roof, she had to discipline herself not to show fear. [5320]

The Orchard was the scene of many extended family gatherings until the girls were grown. Ethel's sister Rosalie Sturges Carpenter and her husband had built a large home on the lake next to Snug Harbor. Their son and daughter were about the same age as the Dummer girls. Because Ethel and Frank Dummer had both come from large families, they had many relatives. Nieces, nephews, cousins and other friends came out from Chicago to join in the many activities Lake Geneva afforded.

In 1902 the Dummers decided to build a third home in Coronado, California, across the bay from San Diego. In 1888 the George Sturgeses, Ethel's parents, had traveled by train with other Midwesterners for the opening of the Hotel del Coronado. Two Illinois businessmen had purchased the Coronado Peninsula and adjacent North Island for $110,000 in 1885. They dreamed of building a resort hotel that would be "the talk of the Western World" and "the finest watering spot on the Pacific Coast". To recoup some of their cost, they charged $1.00 train fare from Chicago, and then sold lots at public auction. [54]   George Sturges used his connections with Chicago business leaders, including officers of the Santa Fe Railroad, to arrange for a private Pullman car to be hooked onto one of the trains. [55]   Upon arrival the Sturgeses were entranced with the area and returned periodically for visits to the Hotel. Mary Delafield Sturges died during a stay there in 1902. [56]

Ethel and Frank contracted with friends, Chicago architect brothers Irving and Alvin Pond, to design a two-story stucco and timber home for them on Adella Avenue. Built in 1905, it looked out on an inlet of San Diego Bay. Enamored with the mild climate and other amenities, the Dummer family escaped to California periodically from Chicago's cold winters. Ethel's surviving brother and two of her sisters soon followed their example, building homes in Coronado and San Diego. During these visits, the Dummer girls had a part-time tutor for their academic studies. But the family also took advantage of the numerous seaside activities such as swimming in the ocean or the Hotel's salt-water plunge and exploring sea life among the rocks at low tide. One year they took a gun boat trip to the nearby Coronado Islands at the invitation of a naval officer friend from Chicago. The girls had horses, kept in the carriage house at the bottom of a sloping lawn, which they could ride around the still developing community. They enjoyed the ferryboat ride from San Diego to Coronado. One year they had a special treat: L. Frank Baum read stories from his Oz books to children at the beach. During visits in the early 1900s, Baum and his wife came from Chicago, like the Dummers, to enjoy Coronado's milder climate.

---

54   Ethel Mintzer Lichtman *History of Sturges Family Descendants,* p. 1; San Diego; unpublished manuscript for the San Diego Historical Society; material in the Coronado Historical Society.
55   Alan W. Johnson, *William Templeton Johnson – the Man and His Works,* chapter 4, p. 7, San Diego; unpublished manuscript
56   *History of Sturges Family Descendents in San Diego,* by Ethel Mintzer Lichtman, for the San Diego Historical Society, 1995

Oz lovers will be interested in a fact from a recent article about Baum's visits. The origin for the character H.M. Wogglebug T.E., a pompous human-sized bug introduced in The Land of Oz, was a crab on the Coronado beach. (H.M. stood for "highly magnified" and T.E. for "thoroughly educated.") [57]

The Dummers of course had staff to maintain their homes and support their life style. Siegfried and Anna, a couple they had brought back from Sweden, were household helpers for many years, Siegfried as custodian who also helped pay household bills, and Anna as cook. Gus Rosenberg, a retired railroad mechanic, was the long-time family chauffeur. Frank Dummer hired him in 1906 when he purchased a car for a trip across country to their new house in Coronado. Gus was like a member of the family as he provided transportation for the Dummer's many excursions, and for Ethel Dummer, who never learned how to drive. (Grandchildren remember Gus telling them that he could take a train engine apart and put it back together, which may or may not have been true. He had worked for the railroad before coming to the Dummers.) Gus and Anna accompanied the family when they stayed in Lake Geneva or Coronado. After Ethel Dummer's death in 1954, Siegfried and Anna, who had lived behind the Dummer home on Michigan Ave., were left a small cottage in Coronado.

The Dummer parents and daughters continued to spend time closer to home, particularly during warmer weather, enjoying the amenities offered at the Orchard. As the girls grew older they put on ambitious dramas such as Shakespeare's *Midsummer Night's Dream* or plays they had written themselves. (After the girls married and grandchildren arrived, The Orchard continued to be a summer gathering place for the extended Dummer and Carpenter families.) But as the

girls became teenagers, family vacation trips went farther afield. Summer dramatics, swimming, and horseback riding at Lake Geneva were followed by trips in the West. With Gus at the wheel, the family went motor camping from Coronado to the Columbia River in Washington State. One year they spent a month at a dude ranch in Wyoming. On

---

57   *The San Diego Union-Tribune*, June 4, 2000

a three-week trip to Yellowstone National Park in 1912, three young men who were close friends of the family accompanied the Dummers. As part of their education, the seven young people took turns writing in a journal each day. It is filled with vivid accounts of spectacular scenery, fishing, horseback riding, baseball for exercise at the end of long days riding, and nights around a campfire.

Equipment for the trip, picked up in mid-July, included a cook-wagon, a dining tent, four sleeping tents with beds and mattresses (the third daughter nicknamed "Happy" expressed disgust with that luxury), a cook and a horse wrangler. Each of the Dummer girls had their own specially made saddle. One journal entry reported that they encountered a large group of coaches filled with tourists. As coach after coach passed, the "real dudes" looked over the Dummer group enviously and made numerous remarks about horseback riding being the <u>real</u> way to see the Park. Accounts of other days record everyone pitching in to help when one of the wagons broke down fording a river, strategies to elude occasional night-time visits by bears, and a campfire discussion "setting the destiny of the human race" while watching the moon rise. [58]

Family pictures of a motor camping trip to California's Crater Lake in 1915 reveal Ethel Dummer's domestic side. Dressed in a traveling suit and decorated straw hat, one shows her flipping flapjacks for breakfast. In another she is darning a sock on Katharine, stretched out on a blanket in front of her. This love of outdoor adventure became instilled in the Dummer daughters and future generations. "Learning by doing" became a focal point of the progressive education which the Dummers came to espouse.

Community Switchboard: 1912-1920

As the second decade of the 20th century progressed, Ethel Sturges Dummer's metamorphosis broadened. While continuing to work with school community centers, her interests and activities to support them branched out to include improving education, parent education and

---

58   Family records

community support of schools, as well as feminism and the problems of women,

She was finding that connecting ideas and people brought action with slight expenditure of effort on her part. Her husband gave her the label of "switchboard", likening her to the telephone operators of the time who connected callers to those with whom they wanted or needed to talk. As her interests expanded with new knowledge, experience, and contacts, Ethel saw an increasing need to bring together people who made and influenced decisions at all levels, from families to political leaders. Today we might call it networking. She wanted to educate herself, but also others who, she realized, saw problems from the perspective of partial facts limited by their interest and experience. Education for a broader understanding of issues and problems became an underlying component of her leadership style in the "professional" part of her life.

While Ethel Sturges Dummer was continuing to help expand The City Welfare Exhibits, and the day and evening programs sponsored by the public schools through auspices of the Women's Club, she kept in touch with what was happening outside Chicago. Social centers with varying purposes were appearing throughout the country, including Cincinnati, Ohio, and Louisville, Kentucky. In 1914 Edward J. Ward of Wisconsin, managing editor of the fledgling *Social Center Magazine*, thanked Mrs. Dummer for supporting their new publication. Its goal was to promote rational appeal in settling individual differences at a time when suspicion and fear were rampant in some neighborhoods, he said. The group launching the magazine had an article from President Woodrow Wilson, the support of his daughter -- the "first maiden in the land"-- as well as an article from former President Theodore Roosevelt endorsing the social center idea and program. Ward gave a talk the following year on "Community Centers for National Defense and World Adjustment" to the American Civic Association. He and other writers were stressing the importance of education for citizenship. [59]

---

59   # 323, Dummer Collection. This source shows the extent of centers beyond Chicago, including a 1911-1912 Survey of School Social Centers throughout the U. S. by the Russell Sage Foundation

Ethel had read an item by a Dr. Golick on the social value of "encouraging the beautiful dances of people who come to America" [60], like those she had fostered and watched at the Kinzie school. That experience two evenings a week had expanded her understanding of slum conditions. She began to examine the role of mothers, unmarried as well as married, to think about human relationships, and to study laws affecting women. Universities educate for every profession except the almost universal one of parenthood, she realized. It was important to put into schools much that was not found in homes. To help others understand this issue, she wrote Dr. Adolph Meyer, Psychiatrist-in-Chief at Johns Hopkins Hospital, for reprints of his talk to the National Conference of Social Workers titled "Organizing the Community for the Protection of Mental Health", which she then circulated to parents and teachers. [61]

Parent education, helping parents become more effective, became one of Dummer's causes. Meeting Chicago Superintendent of Schools Ella Flagg Young one day at the home of a friend, Ethel was surprised to hear her comment that childhood was a very unhappy period, and that physical malnutrition and the kind of emotional disturbances found by Dr. Healy were not the only causes. The majority of children, Superintendent Young said, lacked interests and opportunities. To try to help parents of young children understand the relationship between their child's interests and learning at home and at school, in 1913 Young had introduced in public schools three courses of lectures for mothers by women doctors. Ethel tried to find someone who would expand this effort, who would go with their Child Welfare Exhibit to talk to parents, teaching them how to play with their children. But she could find no one adequate to teach the kind of play that would stimulate creative thinking and learning.

When Ella Young was not re-appointed Superintendent, Dummer believed it important to arouse Chicago citizens to the needs of children, to an interest in the type of education Young had been seeking to secure. At Dummer's instigation, a small luncheon of

---

60   Ibid
61   Dummer Book, pp. 35-38; #230, Dummer Collection

club presidents generated interest in the problem. A larger gathering followed in 1916, at which The Joint Committee on Education was launched. The organization's purpose: to arouse intelligent interest in the public schools and to show the good things schools were doing. Ethel hoped the new organization could be seen as a cooperating group to study education problems throughout the city, not a political group. As background material, with her usual practice of thorough research, she wrote to the United States Commission on Education requesting its annual reports for 1914 and 1915. [62]

The forty-one groups sending delegates to the first meeting of the Joint Committee on Education (JCE) included representatives not only of women's clubs but also of public school teachers and principals. Dummer chaired the group's program committee. Other members of the JCE spread the word in a variety of ways. Mrs. J. Paul Goode, chairman of the sub-committee on school visiting, put out a leaflet showing what to look for when observing a school. No two women's clubs needed to plan the same program or activities. A group studying modern education methods met for book reviews in a room at the public library, where the librarian kept them supplied with the books they wanted. Publicity chairman Mary McDowell secured a weekly column on public schools in the *Record Herald* written by William L. Chenery, in cooperation with the JCE.

In his first column headed "Chicago Women Unite to Help Public Schools", Chenery described the Committee. The organization's purpose, he attributed to Dummer, is to discover and emphasize all of the good things the public schools had already developed. They would not be controversial, and would invite all factions and groups to unite in the undertaking. "We wish to create that public opinion which will demand the best possible public schools for Chicago", he quoted Ethel Dummer. To accomplish this, she believed that Chicago needed to have the support of public opinion; taxpayers must believe in good schools so thoroughly that they would demand the necessary expenditures. The article included Dummer's statement that the new Committee would have no preconceived ideas of what ought to

---

62   Dummer Book, pp. 66/67, Dummer Collection #325

be done. Rather they desired to organize the group so that "natural questions may be answered in the best way". [63]

When Shoop succeeded Young as Chicago's Superintendent of Schools in 1915, Ethel was concerned that new members of the Board of Education had no understanding of the social or community use of the schools. Allen Pond, a Sturges friend interested in civic progress, suggested that she take up the social center situation with the new superintendent. Feeling at first that she might be *persona non grata* because of her friendship with his predecessor, Dummer decided to call on Shoop to explain the City Welfare Exhibit project she and her husband had helped develop, with maps pinpointing community services. She explained that the maps were being offered to eighth grade teachers in schools where the principals approved. Shoop not only proved to be interested, he asked her advice about the community center work being carried on by Edward Burchard at the Harrison High School.

What followed is another example of the approach Ethel Dummer was developing to broaden knowledge and gain the support of decision-makers for solutions to key social issues. She suggested to Shoop that if the president of the school board and members of its committee on community centers would attend a dinner, she would invite those most active in working on social problems and make the arrangements. Early in 1916 eighteen people sat at a round table at the Union League Club, with a skilled social worker alternating with a board guest to permit interaction. Then, beginning with Shoop and going around the table, each person was asked to express his or her opinion. One after another, the board members gave their approval. The vice president, who had claimed there was no legal right to spend school money for such purposes, claimed he had not been adequately informed and withdrew his objection. As guests said good night, the woman board member asked Dummer "How could this have happened when these men fought like cats and dogs at the board meeting?" Dummer attributed her success to the underlying spirit of the proceeding. She had wrestled with herself to control her antagonism toward the board

---

63   #328, Dummer Collection

members until she could invite them in a genuine spirit of wanting them to be her guests. [64]

Shoop thanked Ethel for arranging the meeting, anticipating that it would result in better understanding and a more cooperative spirit. "We are indebted to you for this, but another of the many ways in which you have given of the best of your life to the cause of community center work". [65] The next month the school board raised the appropriation for social centers from ten to forty thousand dollars for the year. Eventually the Board of Education appropriated $150,000 for the community centers. (The centers were developed so fast that standards eventually suffered; by 1938 they were left out of the budget.) [66]

With the support of the Board of Education, Shoop authorized equipping four schools with manual training apparatus and teachers to instruct children in various vocational activities, as well as lunchroom attendants and a supervising teacher for each school. Showers, for parents as well as children, were also provided. Volunteers helped with such classes as drama and sewing. According to Mrs. W. H. Winslow, education chair of the Chicago Women's Club, the plan to keep children off the street and happy in congenial occupation was well worth the effort expended by the Board of Education. "The harvest which will be reaped by the community in consequence of this effort", she declared, "will be a generation of worthwhile citizens". [67] The influence of the women in the JCE was beginning to spread.

A number of districts began to form community councils. A letter to the editor urged newspapers to help spread the word that the Board of Education had a broad policy allowing use of school buildings free with approval of the principal and Superintendent. "You will agree we could not ask more of our cooperative school authorities." But the community needed to organize and apply for this expanded use of facilities. "It will be the wide-awake community that gets the

---

64   Dummer Book, pp. 42-44
65   #311, Dummer Collection
66   #316, Dummer Collection
67   #335, Dummer Collection

privileges". [68] Community centers were being touted as one of the best ways of preparing Americans for democracy. In 1917 Chicago hosted the National Community Center Conference. "Practical Patriotism Demands an Efficient Community", the event notice declared, as it announced three days of activities to help "Develop Your Highest Community Leadership". [69]

While Ethel was busy working to help improve the schools, another part of her mind was occupied with a related interest. She was distressed by what fear and the sense of sin seemed to be doing to children. She wrote Dr. Meyer in 1916 telling him about the new Joint Committee on Education. As program chairman, she told him, to help arouse greater interest and more intelligent opinion concerning modern methods of education, she shared with him her plan to have a group of scientists show what modern thought was contributing to educational theory and method. "Your name came to mind as having not only wisdom but vision." Could he "put in terms of his science a basis of ethics that should be more permanent than the old dogma of fear?" she asked. She wanted to hear a biologist, a psychologist, a sociologist and a psychiatrist speak on the needs of children. "I tried one or two biologists but they both thought I wanted sex education and did not get my point", she told Meyer. It was not cure of problem children so much as maintaining health and securing the right growth and development; not merely sex education which would avoid later complexes, but an environment and opportunity that would make for a more abundant life. Meyer agreed that she would find it hard to get a reputable biologist to open his mouth on education. She urged Dr. Meyer to give a presentation at the lecture series she planned by telling him "Our need is so great in Chicago that I am rather taking it for granted you will come." He agreed to participate "as a contribution in appreciation of the great help you have rendered to the cause of learning more about facts so as to guide good intentions." [70]

Dummer finally found a biologist to join the group. Professor Herbert S. Jennings was reported to have said "If the dear ladies want me to talk

68   #319, Dummer Collection
69   #311, Dummer Collection
70   Dummer Book; pp 68 – 71, Dummer Collection #667

on the young human animal, I'll take a try at it." Dummer believed that his paper "The Biology of the Young Child" showed a goal still far ahead of the times. It fitted exactly with the Dummer's ideals for their daughters twenty years earlier. An assistant superintendent of Chicago schools subsequently referred to the Jennings lecture as his educational bible.

The JCE offered a series of lectures and discussions open to the public. The final course of four lectures titled "Suggestions of Modern Science Concerning Education" was held at the City Club, with co-operation and approval of Superintendent Shoop, in February and March of 1916. Presenters and their subjects were:

> Biology - The Biological Foundation for Education; What Nature Gives to the Children, and the Development of Her Gifts, by Herbert S. Jennings, Johns Hopkins University;

> Psychology - Practical and Theoretical Problems in Instinct and Habit, by John B. Watson, John Hopkins University;

> Psychopathology - Mental and Moral Health in a Constructive School Program, by Dr. Adolph Meyer, Johns Hopkins University;

> Sociology - The Philistine, the Bohemian, and the Creative Man, by William I. Thomas, University of Chicago. [71]

Ethel Dummer was pleased that attendance at this last series of lectures filled the room and included "leading educators and university people". Flora Cooke, principal of Chicago's progressive Francis Parker School, reported her faculty found Meyer's paper to be the most helpful they had ever read. The talk with its charts showing the individual child's life development gave them an understanding of the child's behavior,

While the MacMillan Company did not see the educational value of the series, they printed it in 1916 at Dummer's request and expense,

---

71   #233, Dummer Collection; *Women Building Chicago* ..., p. 236

with no publicity or general advertising. The forward by Ethel Sturges Dummer explained that some mothers were convinced schools hampered rather than helped little children during the years they were acquiring knowledge and developing their natural instincts. "Why, during the years when life is largely sensation", it argued, "do we screw our children into desks for five hours a day?" Might not these four scientists "offer suggestions concerning a school program which should secure physical, mental, and moral health and the development of individual initiative and creative power?"

Within a year the edition was exhausted, challenging the MacMillan Company's view that it lacked educational value. A letter from Patty S. Hill, Director of Kindergarten Education at Columbia University's Teachers College, said she found the booklet very useful in spreading the gospel of the new education among teachers and parents. She considered one or two of the lectures "epoch making". Every member of her large summer session class desired to own a copy, quickly exhausting the supply at MacMillan. She wrote Dummer urging her to have a new edition printed. "I hope I am not intruding in urging this upon you, but realize that you would not have had it published in the first place, had you not been more than eager to help in the cause of education". She is sure that the sale of the book would continue, leaving no financial deficit. The Jennings article, she told Dummer, was the only thing in print that explained the atmosphere they tried to have in early school grades. [72] Twenty-seven years later, in 1944, ESD wrote Frank W. Hubbard of the National Education Association, saying it would be a delight to have him quote from *Suggestions of Modern Science Concerning Education.* She told him that three editions had been brought out in 1920, 1921 and 1925. "It is a great satisfaction to me that the National Education Association now finds value in this book".

Dr. Healy wrote a "splendid review" recommending *Suggestions of Modern Science Concerning Education.* A psychiatrist at the head of a child guidance clinic told Healy he had made a complete digest of the papers in the series. So much for a leading publisher's view of forward

---

72   Ibid "   "

thinking educators of the time! "The Bureau of Educational Experiments also found it of great value", recalled Dummer, "and it is my hope that public school systems may yet discover it." The Jennings article in the publication was followed twenty years later by his *Biological Basis of Human Nature*, "much to the satisfaction of an old grandmother", Dummer tells us in her book.

While continuing her organizational activities, Ethel Dummer was helping the Chicago schools in another way. She provided financial support to selective individuals who she felt were contributing constructively and significantly to keep citizens informed about their schools. Edward Burchard was one of them. She had provided funds for several years for his work as an education specialist with the Extension Civic Welfare Program. A 1916 letter seeking her continued support for the "independent, creative, experimental work" for which she had been giving him free scope reveals his approach to receiving her largesse, as well as the nature of their relationship. It was because of her enthusiasm for humanitarian work and for carrying it out in fundamental and far-reaching ways, he wrote her, that he could accept her personal financial support. Had he felt that her support was only philanthropy or was merely patronizing him, or that it interfered with his other education responsibilities, he told her, he could not have accepted it. She had let him develop his own field, asking only for results, and she gave him ample credit and recognition for those results. He believed that she was helping all those involved in their common effort, according to their respective abilities, to "push along human development as befitted a democracy", he told her. [73]

Ethel continued to arrange for speakers and circulate copies of their reports. The Joint Committee on Education presented committee reports at their annual meeting on May 19, 1917. The one on "Inequalities of Educational Opportunities" included recommendations to be presented to the Board of Education; the report of the Teacher Preparation Committee was deferred to October. In November 1917, Ethel Dummer became ill. Because of her illness and the fact that people were turning to war work, Ethel was unable to find a chairman

---

73   #310, Dummer Collection

to take her place. So the Joint Committee on Education ceased to function. [74]

Evolving Views of Feminism, Motherhood, & Prostitution

In her book *The Grounding of Modern Feminism*, women's historian Nancy F. Cott states that the word feminism is not tied to a specific time in history. Over time it had different meanings to different people. She identifies two ideas dominant within feminism at the beginning of the 20th century's second decade: the emancipation of women as human beings and as sex-beings. [75] Women were challenging the patriarchal family. What Cott refers to as nineteenth century evangelical Protestantism supported the notion that women, considered morally superior to men, encouraged contributions to social life. The feminism that replaced the "woman movement" of earlier years gathered momentum, much of it in the labor and suffrage movements. Leading factions of the "new" feminists were Addams, Julia Lathrop, and Dr. Alice Hamilton, as well as Florence Kelley and Katherine Anthony. Kelley, Director of the National Consumers' League, was the architect of labor and social reform. She and her three children had lived for awhile at Hull House during the 1890's. Together with Julia Lathrop of the Children's Bureau, Kelley helped lobby for laws such as the Maternity and Infancy Act. In 1915 during the First World War, Addams and Hamilton gained prominence as members of the Women's International League for Peace and Freedom.

As we shall see, Ethel Dummer's interests and activities coincided with four of the five women Cott singles out as influential, the exception being Kelley. Dummer worked, sometimes quite closely, with these and other influential women, as well as with men, on behalf of women and children. As a trustee of Hull House (HH) Dummer was in close contact with Jane Addams, particularly in connection with HH-based organizations of their shared interests. In a 1915 note thanking Dummer for giving her a copy of Dr. Healy's book, for example, Addams commends Dummer for her work in establishing the pioneer

---

74   Dummer Book, pp. 71/72; #345, Dummer Collection
75   *Grounding of Modern Feminism,* Cott, p. 49, Yale Press, 1987

psychopathic clinic at the Juvenile Court - "one of the most substantial pieces of work in that field". [76]

A trip to Europe in the winter of 1913-14 gives a good account of how the Dummers blended their family and personal interests. In addition to enjoying the sights and experiences of England and the Continent with their daughters, Frank Dummer wanted to pursue his interest in housing, transportation, and city administration, and Ethel her interest in legislation affecting women and children. Without consulting her, Dummer friend Alan Pond had obtained a letter from the State Department introducing Ethel to U.S. diplomatic and consular officers in Europe. The letter indicated her interest was studying educational methods, particularly with regard to delinquent and "defective" children. [77] Dummer used it to gain entree to hospitals, juvenile courts and people who could give her information on laws concerning women and children. In France she was heartened to find one example of more appreciation for concerns of women and children than she had generally seen in America, with exceptions such as Young's recent lectures in public schools. She located and attended a course on the care of children, free to all women, at an orphan asylum in Paris. When nearly two hundred women and girls arrived for the first class, it was announced that ten other courses would be held in various parts of the city.

In Germany Ethel found a small group of radical feminists who were challenging the patriarchal family, trying to reform marriage, claiming equal rights for all children and the free choice of women to bear children. They believed that love without children might be a constructive spiritual force. After difficulty tracking down the group's leader, Dr. Helena Stocker, she finally obtained an interview. Sitting in Stocker's book-lined study, Dummer found this philosopher open to new ideas about ways "women might climb to a future, which would refuse to permit the wastage of (their) lives." Ethel believed that America might be more ready for Stocker's message than Germany, where women – wives at least - were still in marked subjection to men.

---

76 #420, Dummer Collection
77 #229, Dummer Collection

Dr. Stocker claimed motherhood as the right of every woman, but also that love without parenthood was justified if it enhanced the life of a woman, making for creative power of art and literature. She advocated discovering what marriage laws would ensure an ever-finer next generation. [78]

Ethel Dummer next traveled to Norway to seek out Herr Castberg, the Minister of Justice. Dr. Stocker believed that Castberg's pending bill was the best on the status of children born out of wedlock. With her letter from the State Department, Herr Castberg granted an interview. He went over provisions in the bill that he was introducing that would secure justice for these children. According to his bill, which became law in Norway on January 1, 1915, the name of the father must be given at the time the birth is registered. A guardian for each child born out of wedlock was appointed by the State Board of Control, which was responsible for seeing that the child received care and education according to the status of the more well-to-do parent. One section of the bill bothered Dummer. It freed a legal wife from marriage, if she desired, on discovering that a child was born to her husband by another woman. On thinking this over, Ethel felt that would lower the standard of morals for women and diminish the family as the unit of society.

Returning to America with a copy of the Castberg bill, Ethel Dummer at first felt that settlement workers, probation officers and all interested in the Juvenile Court would surely be ready to accept such legislation. She soon realized, however, that she was overly optimistic, that she lacked the courage to undertake a campaign for similar justice at home. [79] Though her initial attempts to find some group to launch a bill failed, she did not give up the cause.

With her central role in founding the Juvenile Psychopathic Institute, her service as a trustee on several civic and social service organizations, and her trip to Europe, Dummer's reputation as knowledgeable about women's and children's issues began to spread. In the fall of 1916 she

---

78   Dummer Book, pp. 56-60
79   #431, Dummer Collection

received a request from the Chicago Kindergarten Institute, the first training school that accredited kindergarten teachers, to give one of a varied series of lectures under the auspices of the Men's City Club. The Institute's director explained to Dummer the purpose of the lecture series. Our intent, he told her, is to arouse public interest in women's rapidly changing place in society, their sphere of usefulness and education in both home and civic responsibilities. Though Ethel did not yet feel confident about her ability as a speaker, she could not pass up this opportunity to share her message with a wider audience. Asked to state her fee for speaking, Dummer concluded her acceptance letter with the revealing comment: "The fact of having been offered remuneration for such service tickles me to my toes. The only other way I ever earned any money was by weeding my mother's lawn. You will know better than I the fee for such service".

In her talk Dummer described the varying types of feminism found in different countries: the struggle for the vote in England and America, and the quite different effort in Germany and Scandinavia to secure deeper understanding of love, marriage and human rights as distinct from legal rights. "Very shortly we women shall have won the franchise and great personal freedoms", she reminded her audience. She then went on to share her views on the ideal marriage and the role of a mother. "Are we selfishly to enjoy them (our children) or will the maternal instinct carry us into this great movement to secure justice for all children? The finest feminism is that which seeks to solve the problem of mating and motherhood. We must hold ourselves to the highest sexual ideal we can conceive, but never ridicule the conditions of others". [80]

Her notes for the talk show that she first gave her audience a summary of the subject, hoping to help them solve problems of motherhood that they would encounter. She cited Englishman W. L. George as saying that the greatest war being waged in the world was that between the sexes for supremacy. Dummer then referred to some virulent feminists in England and America who would wrest the guidance of the city and country from male control. She spoke of a world movement of women

---

80 Dummer Book, p. 64

toward freedom and mentioned "radical feminists" who wanted to change marriage laws and safeguard motherhood. And she shared the experiences that had led her from her "trim and orderly garden" to the "jungle" of poverty and ignorance, and to what she called her more radical phase of feminism

Explaining her custom of looking at all sides of controversial issues, Dummer pointed out that tangles of poverty, ignorance, selfishness and passion occasionally showed examples of self-sacrifice, loyalty, endurance and courage, challenging one's ideas of right and wrong. She described the work of Maud Miner in New York who was reclaiming hundreds of "fallen women". And she described her own contribution to the work of the Juvenile Protective Association: protesting against forcing marriage to make a child legitimate. She had insisted that two persons parenting a child where there was no caring or love would result in unhappy children and a mockery of marriage. She also shared her belief that vice is largely the result of ignorance or fatigue, pointing out there is a great difference between vice and crime.

Dummer then went on to describe how she had come to believe that human behavior is rooted in biology, the science which many people of her time thought dealt with infinitesimal organisms. The great world need in the light of biology, she told her audience, was the education of parents, reiterating her belief: "we educate for every profession under the sun but the almost universal one of parenthood." She urged reading Katherine Anthony's book *Feminism in Scandinavia and Germany* to gain insight on helping to solve problems of the coming generation; then she described her reasons for supporting the Castberg Bill. During discussion following her talk, Dummer emphasized to young people in her audience that they should not misinterpret her and conclude that the struggle for love's freedoms meant free love. [81]

In reading Katherine Anthony's book, copies of which she circulated among selected contacts, Dummer was particularly interested in a report of a sweeping order that the German Government had adopted. After the war, all children of soldiers were to be made legitimate,

---

81   # 232, Dummer Collection

thereby granting pensions for the mothers. She invited Miss Anthony to Chicago to give a series of talks on women and children's rights. It was the beginning of yet another long association with women activists. The Anthony-Dummer correspondence about their mutual interests spans the years 1916 to 1953, shortly before the latter's death. As a result of Anthony's Chicago talks, four clubs asked Dummer to help write a bill to be presented to the next legislature. The women faced formidable obstacles. An amendment to the Illinois Vital Statistics Act stated that both parents of a child born out of wedlock need not be registered. And in a state with a law permitting a man to disinherit his legitimate child, it was unlikely the legislature would pass a law requiring him to acknowledge an illegitimate child.

The women decided that the first step needed was an education campaign. With Dummer's financial support, Julia Lathrop had the Children's Bureau translate the Castberg Law. [82]

The women's group then disseminated 5,000 copies, with a brief explanation, throughout the country. Dummer wrote judges who indicated interest after receiving the information, suggesting that a "quiet, thorough campaign of enlightenment on the subject" would enable a better measure to be introduced to the next legislature. She also invited them to speak to women's clubs. Meanwhile the Illinois Commission on Social Legislation, with broad representation of many organizations, helped to consolidate the many efforts to introduce legislation on illegitimacy being generated by the women's widespread campaign. [83]

In a 1917 letter to a friend Dummer describes the campaign by women's groups to build support for the Castberg bill. They put the translated copy in the Bulletin of the Illinois Federated Women's Clubs, and they were circulating it and a bibliography of the whole subject of feminism to women's clubs throughout the country. Julia Lathrop also prepared a digest of legislation on the subject for distribution in the U.S. and abroad. In addition, Dummer hoped to secure articles for technical

---

82   # 634, Dummer Collection
83   #369, Dummer Collection

journals. Examples could include an article by Professor Thomas of the University of Chicago for the Journal of Sociology, one from a University of Pennsylvania professor for the Journal of Criminal Law and Criminology, and one from another professor for the Journal of Ethics. They would also try to get an article giving the women's point of view in the *Women's Home Companion* and *The Ladies Home Journal.* It is unclear what parts of this ambitious plan were carried out.

Meanwhile war clouds continued to gather in Europe. Dummer understood that activities of the Red Cross and the Defense Department were likely to detract from interest in the Castberg Bill, but she believed that the publicity might be timely "with the European situation". The whole problem of motherhood and the relationship of the child to the state needed scientific consideration, she told Anthony. In another letter to Anthony she says "If only I had your gift of language I should be writing open letters to the *New Republic* about once a fortnight. Why may we not have a national service offering adequate training and work for women, under scientific supervision?" [84]

While planning how she would help develop support for the Castberg bill, Ethel continued to expand support for women and children in other ways. One of them was working with Julia Lathrop, who was becoming an increasingly influential social worker and reformer. Lathrop had become the second resident at Hull House in 1890; and she had been instrumental in obtaining the grant that created The Chicago School of Civics and Philanthropy (which in 1920 became the University of Chicago's School of Social Service Administration). The Dummer-Lathrop correspondence spans the years from 1912 to 1931; but they also undoubtedly saw each other frequently. Except for the years she spent in Washington D. C. as Chief of the Children's Bureau at the Department of Labor, Lathrop made Hull House her permanent home until her death in 1932. [85]

The Dummer-Lathrop letters show their collaborative relationship as they worked on common interests. One example, in this case also showing

---

84 #430, Dummer Collection
85 *A Useful Woman –The Early Life of Jane Addams,* by Gioia Diliberto, p. 180; Scribners, N. Y. 1999; *Women Building Chicago. (etc.),* p. 491

Dummer's far-flung philanthropy, is revealed in this excerpt from their correspondence. In the fall of 1916, Lathrop wrote Dummer "Do you want to take a little flier at old-fashioned practical neighborliness with a woman in Wyoming?" She went on to describe a statistical study the Children's Bureau was undertaking of Maternal Mortality and how it related to a case of a woman at a state hospital in Wyoming. The next day she sent Dummer an extract of the Bureau's annual report, though sending it was "outside the rules". Studies of infant mortality in town and country revealed that a large portion of babies die in the first days and weeks of life. It included the suggestion that deaths could be prevented through proper care of the mother before, at, and after the birth of the baby. The report was intended to draw attention to mortality from child bearing and stimulate interest and further local inquiry. A February 1918 letter to Dummer from Katharine Morton, Secretary of the Wyoming Public Health Association, reveals how Dummer followed up on Lathrop's plea for assistance. Ethel made available, through Lathrop, $1,000 if the County Commissioners could be persuaded to employ a visiting nurse. Morton's letter explains how, after much resistance, she eventually obtained approval from a Commission that was slow to undertake anything. She assured Dummer that, if the right nurse could be found, the money could not be spent in a way where results would be more far reaching.

As the country was mobilizing for war, Ethel felt she should be doing her part. She wrote Lathrop at the Children's Bureau, saying each one was wondering what his or her service would be. She requested examination papers for applicants at the Bureau, saying she might offer her services if her "mental equipment" could be used. Though not suggesting office work eight hours a day, she said she would love to work *gratis* on Lathrop's planned Maternity Hospital idea, which was an outgrowth of the maternal and infant mortality report, throughout the West. Lathrop's response: "Dear Lady: What a generous, modest soul! You cheer me very much by your trust in the usefulness of what we are trying to do. Perhaps if you go wandering about the rural world this summer you would take a roving commission to see how mothers get on with their young infants, -- and before their children are born." There is no further word of a roving commission. However, in a

September, 1917 letter Dummer mentions to Lathrop having motored to the Pacific Coast and back with members of her family. She identifies districts in New Mexico and Nebraska where she would love to see the Bureau experiment with the maternity hospital idea.[86]

Ethel Dummer's interest in serving her country was rewarded from another source. That same month and year, she received a letter from Raymond B. Fosdick, Chairman of the War Department's Commission on Training Camp Activities, appointing her to a Committee on Protective Work for Girls. "We have had so many serious complaints both from commanding officers and civilians as to the presence of young girls in the neighborhood of military camps", he explained. Fosdick was particularly interested in exploring reformative work in communities near military camps. Miss Maude Miner of the Probation and Protective Association of New York City chaired the Committee. She stated the purpose of the new group: "To endeavor to secure more adequate protection for women and girls during war time, and to aid in the development of protective and reformative work in the cities where military training camps are located". This seemed to conform to Dummer's ideal of a compassionate approach to the problem.

Dummer joined the seven-member committee that included Mrs. John D. Rockefeller, Jr., and the heads of the Young Women's Christian Association and of the Board of Directors of the American Social Hygiene Association. The War Department provided ample financial support. It included funds to establish a School of Philanthropy in New York with a training course for prospective officers and to cover other expenses until municipal budgets or other sources could cover local costs. The new Committee would not conflict with work being handled by the YWCA, with socializing and girls clubs near military camps. It was to assume responsibility for the protective side of the work, with keeping girls off the streets and putting them in touch with women officers trying to prevent an increase in delinquency. (The War Work Council, a committee of the National Board of the YWCA at the time, had a number of committees dealing with social issues, such

---

86   # 634 & 635, Dummer Collection

as committees on social morality, work for foreign-born women, and work among "colored" women and girls.) [87]

The government had been relying on citizens to close red light districts and urge women to move on. Later the women were taken to detention homes and, in some states, quarantined in venereal disease hospitals without trial. Dummer wrote Julia Lathrop asking for advice on the new committee assignment. On December 7, Lathrop called together a small group to discuss the problem of illegitimacy, preventive measures and legislation. Dummer believed that if earnest efforts could continue to safeguard young persons whose social life was altered by mobilization, the increase in illegitimacy rates could be reduced.

After two months serving on the committee, Ethel Dummer succumbed to an attack of tuberculosis, which sent her to recuperate for some months in the Dummer house in Coronado. Her husband visited and wrote frequently with family news; he also kept her up to date on progress with the Castberg law. [88] Lying on her back, she received monthly reports on the War Department committee from Washington and weekly reports from her Midwest district. Plans were necessarily abandoned to visit camps in her neighborhood with Jessie Binford, a resident of Hull House and superintendent of the JPA, who had been appointed by the Committee on Protective Work for Girls to supervise the country's central district. [89]

While recuperating, Ethel enjoyed the warmer climate and looking down across the sloping lawn watching the sailboats in Glorietta Bay, an inlet of San Diego bay. As she gained strength she took short walks, eventually to the Coronado Hotel about a mile from her home. There she could sit on the veranda watching the surf, or inside in the peaceful, flower-filled courtyard. She kept up her correspondence as much as she could, telling Josephine Perry, her secretary at the time who remained in Chicago, that she felt like a "lame duck" without her.

---

87   # 377 & 378, Dummer Collection
88   #37, Dummer Collection
89   *Women Building Chicago* ....; p 82

Ethel wrote home requesting detailed social case histories of promiscuity. As her strength permitted, she studied them carefully. She felt many cases showed that early sex experience had been treated with a lack of sympathy or understanding. The reports reminded her of the time she had been shocked when she visited the Illinois Industrial School. Unlocking an iron grill a matron had shown her a room full of "very young girls" busy with handwork. When Dummer asked "what on earth are such children doing here?" the matron had replied: "They have had sex experience and must not be permitted to mingle with other children lest they contaminate them." Ethel was also pondering the work of Dr. Healy, who found that a girl may come through a sexual experience psychically unharmed, while another with no physical experience, obsessed with ideas about sex, can be far more difficult to rehabilitate. And she remembered an article by a German major saying German criminologists considered that prostitutes were feebleminded and could live no other way. There was much to think about. [90]

A number of professionals throughout the country were also pondering the sexual aspect of problems with adolescent girls and women. Some saw these women as using their sexuality for economic and social gain. The issue became blurred, states Kyle Emily Ciani in her article on "Problem Girls". "Was 'feeblemindedness' the cause or effect of female deviancy?" Two groups with different perspectives were seeking solutions to the problem of unmarried mothers: evangelical women who saw illegitimate children as symbols of a sexual double standard, and social workers who saw them as "agents of a larger social problem" who were infecting the security of the family. Ethel Dummer seems to have partially bridged the gap between these groups. [91]

Dummer received word in California that she had been elected to membership on the Board of the Illinois Society of Mental Hygiene. The executive committee included women with whom she frequently worked: Addams, Hamilton and Lathrop, and Judge Mary Bartelme, recently appointed Assistant Judge at the Juvenile Court. [92] Ethel's

---

90   Dummer Book, pp. 80-83
91   *Problem Girls: Gendering Criminal Acts and Delinquent Behavior,* Kyle Emily Ciani, in Journal of Women's History, Vol. 9, No. 3, pp. 204 & 208
92   #358, Dummer Collection

reputation was also spreading in Southern California as she spent several months each year, usually during the winter, at the Dummer house in Coronado. As she regained her strength and professionals became aware of her interests, she made new contacts. Local women protective officers and district supervisors came to discuss problems of venereal disease and related issues with her. While visiting the San Diego Venereal Disease Hospital one day she watched while a new girl brought in with her baby was surrounded by other obviously interested girls. This led Ethel to thinking about child bearing as a fundamental function of women. Apparent "feeblemindedness", she thought, may be the result of shock and scorn. "The stupidity of our past intolerance quite overwhelms one", she wrote a friend, "when one visits the venereal disease hospitals and finds these 'wild women' to be pitiful children, sadly in need of help".[93]

The War Department's Committee for the Protection of Girls was brought under the Law Enforcement Division of the Commission on Training Camp Activities. Dummer's role, as might be expected from her past activities and due to her illness, was largely to disseminate ideas, what she called the "osmosis of thought". In July 1918, upon receiving Miss Miner's report of the first six months, she wrote approving the policy of trying to establish permanent organizations to continue after the war. With the lack of funds and public interest, however, she reluctantly realized the effort would probably have to be carried on by volunteer groups of social workers. She was disappointed that the Committee's work was focused primarily on negative aspects and law enforcement, which to her implied a return to medical supervision of prostitutes. She fervently hoped to urge a more positive approach, consistent with her thinking. "As through the mating instinct, love, loyalty and self-sacrifice have been evolved, surely it should be interpreted to youth as the most sacred of endowments instead of a curse, fearsome and indecent." Her efforts to convince the physician and lawyer working for the Committee's Interdepartmental Board of this approach were not fruitful. "At that time Mental Hygiene was too new a science. They did not comprehend". ... "The more one learns of conditioned reflexes", she wrote a friend, "the more one dreads the

---

93 Dummer Book, p. 84

results of associating in the minds of thousands of people such horrors of vice and disease with that of life which should be joyous and beautiful". Comments such as this suggest the influence of her relatively sheltered family background. [94]

She continued to stress the importance of case histories, of studying conditions that resulted in "abnormal over-sexualization", believing that condemnation would be replaced by more opportunities for rehabilitation if people understood underlying factors in each case. "Surely among all the doctors at work in the state hospitals for venereal disease, some will become interested in more than the cleansing of the bodies." [95] During periodic times of rest, her brain was at work developing ideas to expand the Committee's work, to secure psychological and sociological data that should be "a distinct contribution to the feminist movement." She realized it would take some years to assemble data on cases to support conclusions of Dr. Healy and others that some cases of law-breaking "misbehavior" were the result of "nature's highest product, a human body". "We must secure for motherhood a marriage law based on biology rather than economics." [96] Extensive reading of reports and studies showed, for example, that red light districts were visited more in college towns during examinations than at any other time of year. Does reaching the limit of fatigue or nerve strain result in lowering inhibitions and self-control? She was surprised to find the number of women married to absent servicemen engaged in illicit relations not for money but from an apparent need to demonstrate and receive affection. Early in the century, when the field of psychology was still young, this reaction was probably less naive than it would be today.

In October 1918 Dummer was pleased to learn that after months of hard work the Army issued orders to psychiatric units to examine all girls for venereal disease in detention houses and isolation hospitals. She hoped these results of the Committee's work would add to the growing body of thinking about prostitution. At the All American Conference on Venereal Disease in Washington D.C. in December

94   Dummer Book, pp. 85/86
95   Dummer Book, pp. 90
96   Dummer Book, pp. 86/87

1920, Miss Miner, Ethel Dummer, Jessie Binford and others who had worked on the Committee on Protective Work for Girls presented resolutions making two recommendations:

1. To abolish compulsory exams and forcible detention of persons suspected of carrying venereal disease, and replace these practices with adequate facilities for voluntary examinations, treatment and constructive re-education;

2. To appoint a committee to include a biologist, psychologist, psycho-pathologist and sociologist to study whether there is scientific basis for attacks on marriage; if so, to determine what law based on biology and psychology rather than economics might tend to "secure to humanity the highest values evolved in human love, together with ever increasing social health". [97]

To the distress of both Dummer and Minor, regulations based on the results of the committee's work were placed under a law enforcement department. It looked like not much attention was given to their second recommendation. Disappointed, Miss Minor resigned. [98]

Excerpts from letters and other items in the Dummer Collection give additional insight to Ethel Sturges Dummer's thoughts and opinions on feminism, motherhood and prostitution during this period. In an undated, twelve-page paper about women and marriage titled "Some Thoughts on Life and Love", Dummer comments: "We must recognize that for many women marriage is still a slavery. It is natural that the reaction from repression and the sense of the marriage tie as a chain sends women far afield, and we are called upon to reckon with much publicity of unstable emotion and a demand from more than one quarter for free sexual life for women." [99] In another undated, untitled paper on prostitution, she states her discouragement with government arrests of women suspected of venereal disease, and relates her experience gathering histories of young prostitutes and visiting venereal disease hospitals. She indicates that her interpretation of the girls' behavior and

97   #390, Dummer Collection
98   #850, Dummer Collection
99   #236, Dummer Collection

the psychology of prostitution are quite different from what doctors and criminologists were saying at the time. She shares her belief that prostitutes' so-called feeblemindedness more closely resembled wartime shell shock and that re-education was possible.

In practically all cases she had studied, she relates in her book, early sex experience was "stupidly" treated. There was little sympathetic understanding of the bewilderment of children from age 8 to 16 who were "meeting the mystery of life unprepared, -- meeting the physical manifestation unassociated with the psychical values we call love." Psychological values that can be attained during pregnancy and maternity were ignored, while the girl's character was weakened in the effort to hide the fact of motherhood. "Although this was done in an effort to 'save her reputation', it was a sad blunder." [100] Finally, in a 1918 letter Dummer commends Elizabeth MacManus of the Los Angeles City Welfare Bureau for advocating the importance of interpreting the cause and situation in venereal disease cases. If people understood the underlying factors in a case, she explained, condemnation would largely disappear and more opportunities for rehabilitation would be offered these women. [101]

Dummer turned again to Dr. Healy, writing for his reaction to her thinking about the problem of prostitution. The study of the little children back in the Chicago Juvenile Court seemed to her a relatively simple matter compared with the cases of older children that had been left unsolved, particularly of girls where prostitution could result. She suggested that psychiatrists try to work on a solution to prostitution as a next logical step. Studying case reports, she explained, had led her to believe that a percentage of prostitution could be checked by a living wage, but most of all, if public attitudes about early sex education of young girls could be changed. The two of them had earlier agreed that the negative terms "ruined" and "fallen" must be given up. She suggested that use of such crude terms might start girls downhill if they

---

100   #375, Dummer Collection
101   #385-A, Dummer Collection

were made to feel they had committed an "unpardonable sin". Wouldn't sympathetic, understanding treatment, explaining the mystery of life and joy of motherhood be more likely to lead to rehabilitating the girls? She called his attention to the California State Board's humane work attracting men and women suffering from venereal disease to their clinics, comparing it with police arrest driving them away, the practice in other states. And she related the positive approach and apparent successful treatment of feeblemindedness by Freud and other psychiatrists curing blindness and soldiers with shell shock. Inquiring if he knew of any psychiatrists doing special work in the field of prostitution, she added "Why has it taken us two thousand years to understand the teaching of the Great Psychiatrist (presumably Jesus) the message: 'Neither do I condemn thee'?" [102]

Dummer wrote Dr. Meyer seeking advice on young girls' sexual development and sex problems and their relationship to the role of the mother. For many years, he responded, some of his medical students had given him short sketches of their sexual development and sex problems. He had felt obligated to combine the material into a constructive statement for general use. Yet he saw the times as one of turmoil on the subject. Perhaps simply treating problems as they come and drawing general conclusions was best. "Each nation and each social group seems to have its own tenets", he said; "we can fortunately always fall back on the resources of human nature itself." [103]

In October 1919, Dummer attended the International Conference of Women Physicians in New York. Her attempts to expand agenda items to include topics of her interest had been thwarted. Dr. Meyer was to be a speaker at one session; she had hoped to expand his involvement. But being a man, he was not eligible, as she proposed, to attend any other session except by invitation. Dr. Anna L. Brown, YWCA Vice President and Social Education Director who headed the organizing committee, responded to Dummer's request: "I hope that no such effort as you suggest will be made by the Interdepartmental Social Hygiene Board or the American Hygiene Society". It would be quite

---

102   Dummer Book, pp. 91-93
103   #667, Dummer Collection

impossible, she added, for any delegate to the Conference to give any time for meetings other than scheduled sessions. [104]

After the Conference Dummer wrote to a Dr. "M" (presumably Dr. Meyer) about a paper given by Wilfred Lay, "Reinterpretation of Childhood", which had particularly interested her. She expressed sympathy with Lay's thought that repressive punitive methods must be replaced by constructive processes, and his comment "There is no such thing as wholesome fear even of disease. You are right in saying that for any scientific study a wide range of individual solutions must be undertaken", she wrote, "but it does not take more than one case in our morals court to prove to me that present treatment of the young prostitute is unjust, unintelligent, and futile - and womanlike, I want to clean house, or court, at once....It was the knowledge that we must present argument scientifically based that led me to try to interest you in the subject. As the study extends, one sees how far-reaching it may be." [105] Dummer circulated copies of this letter to several physicians and social workers, presumably her reason for not identifying Dr. M.

In undated notes headed "Some Thoughts on Men and Women", Dummer argues that the report of the government's Committee on Prostitution should be given wider attention by a public generally ignorant about young girls suffering from irregular sex relations. "Two years has shown such hope for the rehabilitation of the young prostitute", she states optimistically, "that only the average woman's attitude of mind toward the subject prevents the downfall of prostitution as a big business." In words revealing her convictions and reactions to social trends, she adds "Will not the Mothers of this country bring about a new vision? Let sex be considered sacred instead of indecent, let children feel their power of parenthood as a trust for future generations."

In her thoughts on sex education, Dummer advocated satisfying the natural curiosity of the very little child with scientific knowledge given in an unemotional manner, likening that to the Greeks' reverence of the body so nakedness was admired and respected. A fine body was to

---

104   #388, Dummer Collection
105   Dummer Book, pp. 96-99

be attained if possible, she thought, by careful living, moderation, and self-control.[106] Ethel elaborates her opinion on the subject in a lengthy statement from yet another source. The fact that physical maturity is attained before the full mental and spiritual development necessary for love as an art is attained, she states, may explain the many "mis-matings" of early sex relations within and without marriage. "May we not teach our young people such respect for parenthood that they may gain strength and character by so controlling the urge of adolescence that a greater power is their's later to transmit to children through a union based on congeniality of mind and spirit, more lasting then the mere passing fancy for face and form. We have not evolved to a very high conception of the marriage relations; there still clings to it the idea of ownership of each by the other. .... My conclusion is that women must end prostitution, not by repression or punishment, but by securing methods of education which shall make impossible any sex relation which lacks psychical and social values." [107]

An August 1917 letter from the Juvenile Court's Chief Probation Officer must have given recipient Mrs. W. F. Dummer some satisfaction. On behalf of officers and employees of the Court, he thanks her for signing the indemnity bond. "We will try to express our thanks by doing everything we can for the welfare of the neglected and delinquent children of Cook County. A handwritten note at the end adds: "You deserve a great deal more thanks than anyone else. [108]

Family Nurturer

Despite the satisfaction she undoubtedly derived from favorable responses to her "good works", that couldn't compare to what Ethel Sturges Dummer felt as a wife and mother, watching their three daughters grow into adulthood. During the years she was pursuing her "professional" interests while maintaining three homes, she was certainly not neglecting her immediate and extended family. In a report with information about her for a national honor society in 1944, educator and contemporary Flora J. Cooke described Ethel's home as

106   Dummer Book
107   #375, Dummer Collection
108   #373, Dummer Collection

"the center of her existence and inspiration for her work beyond its gates. Her devotion to her husband and her collaboration with his interests and hobbies is a story in itself, an exceptionally fine example of a delightful and productive human relationship. In her own happy, well-adjusted children she has found the challenge and spur to try to help all children to enjoy wholesome opportunities, making for their full and satisfying development." Dummer had once told Cooke that she found her greatest joy and recreation in "playing with mathematics, poetry and philosophy – and with her grandchildren."

As the four Dummer daughters reached adulthood, they began to adapt what they had learned during their upbringing to match their own interests. When Marion, the eldest, developed an interest in business, her father became her personal trainer; he took her with him on his trips to Europe related to international banking. During her later twenties Marion went to Hollywood for six months and took a job editing film and working in a library. In 1918 she returned to Chicago and married Chicago physician Donald Putnam Abbott. By 1925 the Abbots had three daughters and a son and lived in a house near the University of Chicago.

Katharine, the second Dummer daughter, attended Radcliffe College in Cambridge, Massachusetts. In 1915 she married Harvard graduate and attorney Walter Fisher. They built a large, modern brick home designed by Fisher's architect brother in Hubbard Woods near Winnetka on Chicago's North Shore. When the first two of the Fisher's six children were born, a son and daughter, Katharine started a nursery school in their home. It carried out many of the newer approaches to early childhood learning with which she had been brought up. As her family grew, she became active in the League of Women Voters, founded in Chicago in 1920 – the year women finally obtained the right to vote. Katharine Fisher would later become treasurer of the Illinois League of Women Voters – then an officer of the National League.

Dummer's daughters Ethel (Happy) and Frances entered Francis Parker School in Chicago in 1907 for their high school years. Tutors and their parents had conducted their schooling up to then. The school was founded in 1901 to carry out the educational objectives of Francis W. Parker, head of the School of Education at the University of Chicago. He was a contemporary of John Dewey and other progressive educators. Objectives of the school included preparing students for self-discipline and for growth into "ideal citizenship". The Dummers concurred with a number of its features such as "learning by doing" and the belief that social reform could take place through education. Years later in a 75th birthday letter to Ethel Sturges Dummer, the school's longtime Director Flora Cooke commented that in 1907 she could not have foreseen what the Dummer family would contribute to the educational progress, "not only in the Parker School but to the country from coast to coast, nor that its influence would reach across the seas." [109] After graduating from Parker, the Dummer girls both went on to attend and graduate from the University of Wisconsin.

During this time Ethel and Frank Dummer continued to see that their family activities did not suffer from their busy civic and business interests. While Happy and Frances were in college, Madison was not far from Chicago. The girls made frequent trips home and Gus drove their mother to Madison for visits. All members of the family spent times together at Lake Geneva and Coronado. A happy three-generation family snapshot taken on the lawn in Coronado shows Ethel and Frank holding their first two grandchildren, surrounded by their four daughters. By 1920 four grandchildren had arrived: two Abbotts and two Fishers. Letters from their mother to Happy and Frances in Madison described frequent visits to the Abbott and Fisher homes. Marion and Katharine often brought their children to the four-story Dummer town home to play with their mothers' childhood toys and to climb or crawl up and down the stairs. On evenings when they were not going to meetings, the theater or to friends, Ethel and Frank spent happy hours in front of the fire in the "growlery" reading and talking. (One grandchild living today recalls that name as coming from a favorite children's book.) Ethel's part-time secretary Janet Hall (nicknamed Bunny) helped her with correspondence, giving her more time for family. Hall referred to Ethel as "lady boss". [110]

---

109   #271, Dummer Collection
110   #567, Dummer Collection

Ethel claimed that assimilating three generations was made simple for her because of her husband's love for children. Experience with their own babies had given him insight as a grandfather and a "superb understanding". As the grandchildren grew they readily learned that on visits to the Dummer home, their grandparents were not to be disturbed when they were in their study; otherwise the children's frequent appeals for attention and answers to questions were always welcomed. [111]

Ethel's "tribe" was a large one. She had been born into a prolific family. Her grandparents Solomon and Lucy Hale Sturges had nine children, of whom Ethel's father George was the seventh. George and Mary Delafield Sturges also had nine children. Added to the offspring of George's siblings, the Solomon Sturges grandchildren totaled fifty-three, giving Ethel forty-four Sturges first cousins. She was the eldest of George and Mary Delafield Sturges' six children who lived to adulthood: five daughters and one son. Throughout her life Ethel maintained a close relationship with her five surviving siblings. She also found time to keep in close touch with members of her husband's family. Henry and Phoebe Ness Dummer had five children, including another son besides Frank, and three daughters. Ethel corresponded and kept in touch with them as well as with two of her husband's cousins. The Dummer Collection at the Schlessinger Library includes 84 folders of Ethel's correspondence with members of the Sturges and Dummer extended families, filled with evidence of her close relationship with many of them. A number of the letters show that it was frequently Ethel to whom they came when in need of advice or solace.

Three of Ethel's sisters married and lived in the Chicago area, at least for awhile, as did her brother George Sturges Jr. Like the Dummers who had been drawn to Southern California and built a second home in Coronado, two of Ethel's sisters and her brother George eventually migrated to San Diego, as did the daughter of her Sister Rosalie. Though Rosalie and her husband Hubbard Carpenter remained in Chicago, they spent time in their large house "Reheboth" on the shores

---

111   Dummer Book, pp. 112 & 113

of Lake Geneva, next to the Sturges family home, Snug Harbor. They and their family often shared summer activities with many of the expanded Dummer family at Lake Geneva. Throughout her life Ethel maintained a close relationship with her surviving siblings.

The youngest Sturges child, Clara, was twelve years younger than Ethel and only 23 when their mother died during a visit to the Coronado Hotel. Four years later Clara married William Templeton Johnson, born and raised in Staten Island, New York. She helped encourage and finance his education and training as an architect at the Sorbonne in Paris, where their first son was born. Upon their return to the states, they had planned to live on the East Coast, but a visit to the Dummers in Coronado changed their minds. The visit would lead to these two Sturges daughters having a broad impact on education in San Diego.

Because of a shared interest in education and other social issues, Ethel was probably closest to her sister Clara. In 1910 Clara and her husband (known in the family as "Temp") visited George and the Dummers in their Coronado homes. The Johnsons fell in love with San Diego and decided to settle there. Distressed about the general caliber of schools, the visit with the Dummers led them to decide to found a school in San Diego. It would be a laboratory for some of the education theories of the Dummers, and of Chicago progressive educators Francis Parker and John Dewey. They named it Francis W. Parker School after the school Clara's two nieces, "Happy" and Frances Dummer had attended in Chicago. The school opened in 1912 in a temporary small building in San Diego. They hoped such ideas as learning by doing and field trips, if successful, could be adapted in the then more rigid public schools. Ethel helped the Johnsons recruit the first principal, a high school principal then working in Pasadena, whom the Dummers had met earlier when the latter's family lived in Coronado.

The Johnsons built their first home in Coronado, then a larger house in San Diego to accommodate their anticipated growing family. It was not far from the unusual building for the new school that Johnson designed, built around a courtyard to take advantage of the city's mild climate. With new curriculum as well as architectural features, the school soon attracted attention nationally and beyond. A 1917 local news article called it a "remarkable institution --.....a prophecy of what public schools would become in ten-to-twenty years." [112] A guest book of that time includes names of visitors to the "lab school" from throughout the United States and abroad. Maria Montessori came from Rome with several teachers to see the new school that was testing new theories. Templeton Johnson went on to become a prominent San Diego architect.

After graduating from the University of Wisconsin 1918, Happy went to teach at the new Francis Parker School in San Diego founded by her Aunt Clara Sturges Johnson. Frances soon followed and taught there for several years. The sisters lived in the Coronado house across the bay. Happy would go on to head the San Diego school, while Frances returned to the Chicago area to pursue her education interests.

Frank Dummer's relationship with his daughters was always very close. He was a pioneer in recognizing what his wife referred to in her book as the "psychic contributions" a father could give a family. Instead of ordering and forbidding as a dominating patriarch, he opened new doors to wider interests. When he attended a conference on the Conservation of Natural Resources, for example, he took with him his two oldest daughters, then fourteen and sixteen. Years later one of Ethel's daughters showed her a list of maxims her father had once shared with her. It reveals much about his philosophy of life.

- To curb personal wants which expand easily but shrink with difficulty.

- To be gentle with those who serve, since they are not free to resent.

- To mingle freely with all classes, and thus know mankind.

---

112   Ethel Mintzer Lichtman, "The Francis Parker School Heritage", 1985; & The Historical Resource Center,
Francis Parker School, San Diego.

- To be mastered by no habit or prejudice, no triumph or misfortune.

- To promise rarely, and perform faithfully.

- To choose hobbies with care and pursue them with diligence.

- To be just, man's supreme virtue, which requires the best of head and heart.

By living the ideal "as a man thinketh so is he", Frank Dummer created a personal influence felt by all those around him, according to his wife. [113]

In a 1921 letter to her daughters their mother reveals her feelings about her evolving relationship with them. "You are children no more. You are grown and flown from the nest. It is hard in age to curb emotions of earlier years, to realize that no longer am I to expect to follow your daily doings, your daily welfare. The "mother" in me dies hard, and the "grandmother" has to be kept in control, or else the real grandmotherly spirit has not been developed. It is hard to draw the line between showing enough interest and not showing too much....I cannot get away from a sense of responsibility. Yet I can almost hear strong language as you read of my perplexity. Am I a foolish mother?" [114]

113 Dummer Book, p. 134
114 #166, Dummer Collection

II. Social Philanthropist: 1920-1945

Ethel Sturges Dummer's Evolving Role & Style

How is Ethel Dummer's life perceived now by those who know of her? How was she perceived in her time? In a 1992, article "Acting As A Switchboard: Ethel Sturges Dummer's Role in Sociology", British sociologist Jennifer Platt finds no single name for Dummer's role or roles, though she says the word "patron" could apply. [115] In addition to philanthropist and her husband's label "switchboard", terms used by the few people currently familiar with the "professional" part of Dummer's life include catalyst, social reformer, philosopher, and, in some respects, the more recent term networker.

Platt states that though Dummer's role was significant in the inter-war period, it has largely been forgotten, despite her high level of "professional" activity. She suggests that what she sees as Dummer's modesty about her professional contributions could have been a lack of self-confidence due to not having a college education. She may also have thought she could be more effective if she maintained a more old-fashioned style in some respects, perhaps a dash of *noblesse oblige*. For example, when she wanted to make sure that she reflected the traditional point of view; to some recipients she signed her letters Mrs. W. F. Dummer.

Ethel Sturges Dummer's self-confidence grew as she received increasing recognition for her contributions from some leading professionals.

---

115   Jennifer Platt; <u>American Sociologist,</u> Fall 1992; pp. 23, 28, & 32

Being married to a wealthy man, in addition to having inherited wealth, also gave her the time and means to pursue her philanthropic activities. But money was by no means her only method of furthering the mental health, childcare, and education causes she espoused. Financing and widely distributing copies of books and authoritative papers was a major component of her style. Being appointed program chair and arranging conferences and panels for regional and national organizations was another avenue for her largesse and influence. She thus furthered her efforts and exposure, while securing varying points of view and opinions from sociologists, psychologists, psychiatrists, educators and other professionals. She underwrote research, surveys, courses, and projects, and opened the extensive library in the Dummer home as a meeting place. [116]

Dummer was by no means the only social reformer of her time in Chicago. As the thousand-page book *Women Building Chicago – 1799-1999* attests, 423 social and civic reformers, including Dummer, accomplished a great deal bringing about changes in diverse geographical and interest areas of metropolitan Chicago. [117] This account refers to Dummer as a philanthropist and education and mental health reformer. Carolyn DeSwarte Gifford, women's historian, author and associate editor of *Chicago Women*, who edited the entry on Dummer written by Platt, calls Dummer a "remarkable" woman, particularly because of how she made things happen. Gifford believes that Dummer's personality was crucial to the process. She saw things, looked at problems from a different perspective than most other reformers. Gifford distinguishes Ethel Sturges Dummer from most of her contemporary reformers saying "she was interested in changing systems".

In a nine-page report on Dummer requested by Delta Kappa Gamma National Honor Society in 1944, her contemporary Flora Cooke, educator and principal of Chicago's Francis Parker School describes Dummer's rather

---

116   Dummer Book, p. 126
117   *Women Building Chicago*

"...fixed pattern to her work. First, she seems always to meditate upon a problem presented until she has its objectives clearly in mind and a plan evolved. Second, she seeks out experts wherever they may be (in the United States or abroad) who have most to offer in the particular field in which the problem lies. Third, she solicits and usually obtains the help of these recognized 'experts' who are able to speak with authority on the subject. Fourth, when possible she puts the recommendations she receives to the test of practical use. Fifth, and finally, if any encouraging results are obtained, she starts a campaign to educate the Public to the social values of her findings."

Cooke notes in her report that almost every page in Dummer's autobiography refers to the work of some active committee, casually mentioning herself as a member or chairman of the program committee of the organization sponsoring the project. "It took careful research into the city's civic archives, and into the files of various social agencies and educational institutions, to reveal the fact that not only was Mrs. Dummer an active worker behind the scenes in all these cases – but that nine out of ten times -- the very existence of the welfare project under consideration was due to her initiative, and its continuance, often over a period of years, depended on her generously volunteered financial support, or that of her family, or that of some club she had interested in an issue for the common good." Cooke ends this long statement: "However, it is fair to quote Mrs. Dummer herself, who has often said 'Such work seldom traces to only one person, but gradually develops out of cooperative thinking and the concerted action of a group of interested people". [118]

Mental Hygiene, Delinquent Behavior and Networking

In January 1920 Ethel was appointed to the California State Conference of Social Work's committee on delinquency. It was one of five sections appointed by the conference president Dr. Ray Lyman Wilbur. In a prominent display of Sturges family members new to the region, the section on child welfare was headed by Ethel's sister, Clara Sturges

---

118   Dummer Collection #216

Johnson. The Whittier State School in Orange County housed the Journal of Delinquency, devoted to the scientific study of problems related to social conduct. The school's Superintendent and its Director of Psychology and Research had not met Dummer. However, they had learned about her experience and interests and felt she would be valuable in enacting wise legislation for California. The delinquency section was asked to prepare a program and a statement on the status of delinquency for the next conference. The assignment fit right in with Dummer's interests. [119]

Demonstrating her emerging networking skills, Ethel arranged to have her friend Katherine Anthony read her paper titled The Emotional Basis of Individual Character at the May conference. [120] Pleased that Clara had invited Dr. Alice Hamilton to speak at the meeting of social agencies, Ethel wrote the physician about her deepening interest in rehabilitating prostitutes. She asked for 25 copies of Hamilton's report on the health of prostitutes. Ethel hoped to draw representatives of the American Social Hygiene Society and the International Hygiene Board who attended the meeting into a roundtable discussion that would show how the "law enforcement and lock step method" that followed European regulations had proved a failure. [121]

Like Ethel, Alice Hamilton had been educated at home, brought up in an intellectually stimulating, religious, socially protected environment. She had decided on a career in medicine as one of the few professions open to women at the time. After completing her training, she became a professor of pathology at the Women's Medical School of Northwestern University, where she became an authority on treating industrial diseases. She had become one of the inner circle of women and a close colleague of Jane Addams at Hull House, where she lived at the time. After working for two years for the Bureau of Labor Statistics in the new Department of Labor in Washington D.C., in 1919 Hamilton became the first woman professor at Harvard Medical School, (which became part of Harvard's School of Public Health in 1925), specializing in industrial medicine. The account of Hamilton in

119   Dummer Collection #389
120   C Dummer Collection #434
121   Dummer Collection #382

<u>Notable American Women: the Modern Period</u> calls her a crusader for public health and an advocate for the helpless, a woman who wanted to make the world a better place. [122]

Dummer and Hamilton kept in touch throughout their lives, through personal contact, correspondence, and sharing publications on common interests. It proved to be a fruitful exchange. After reading an editorial in *The New Republic* in 1917 on birth control, for example, Ethel commented to Alice what an uphill struggle it would be, "pushing ahead these rocks of legal and theological tradition which ever roll back upon us. However, it is good fun to be in the game of humanity". In another note Dummer thanks Hamilton for giving her a glimpse of settlement life at Hull House – probably including the effects on health and other social consequences of living in squalor. Through her friend's eyes, Ethel was beginning to see the meaning and importance to the world of preventing industrial disease. When she sent Hamilton reprints of the round table in California on delinquency, the latter responded that she found the discussion so interesting and full of new ideas that she planned to use it in hygiene lectures to college girls. "Isn't it wonderful that the new way of regarding problems concerning the strange conduct of young people is growing rapidly," she asks? She concludes that letter to Dummer: "You have of course done much to bring this about, and indeed there is nothing you could have done that would have been more worthwhile and few things that would bring you as little glory. But I dare to guess that you never thought of that aspect of it." [123]

Dummer continued her practice of disseminating materials as an effective education tool. To help broaden the interest among those dealing with prostitution, she placed 20 copies of books dealing with the subject, selected from her reading and experience, in the San Diego social work office. After they had circulated for two years, a supervisor in the San Francisco office begged for the books to be sent north and Dummer complied. [124] Another example shows the widening scope

---

122   *Notable American Women ...*, (etc.) pp. 306-308; & *Women Building Chicago ...,*(etc.), pp. 345/6
123   Dummer Collection #382
124   Dummer Book, p. 91

of Ethel Dummer's activities and contacts. A letter from a San Diego assistant probation officer asked for her reaction to a manuscript by a local psychologist and philosopher on the nature of sexual activity. He had met her at a national social work conference in San Francisco and wrote: "I meet you everywhere in social work literature and marvel at - and approve of your insight, persistence and ability." [125]

Physicians had shown little interest in Dummer's hunch about the causes of behavior, saying feeblemindedness was feeblemindedness. She believed that women in VD hospitals seemed more bewildered than vicious and wicked. She wondered if women in reformatories couldn't be curable like shell-shocked men after the war. Ethel had been impressed by a little book by Dr. William White titled *Mental Hygiene of Childhood*. When next in Washington she asked White, psychiatrist-in-chief at Saint Elizabeth Hospital of the Department of the Interior, about the possibility of rehabilitating young prostitutes. The subject was growing in her mind, she later wrote him, to look not only at rehabilitation of prostitutes but also at the health of all sex relations, leading to a law of marriage based on biology and psychology rather than on economics. She hoped to put together a conference to stimulate thought on the subject, similar to "Suggestions for Modern Science on Education". She was thinking about getting physicians Healy, Meyer, Bronner and hopefully White to write papers on the subject. "I have fun with my imagination", she told White, "but I try not to let it break lose till its visions have been verified by science." But White told Dummer he was convinced that a large percentage of prostitutes were feebleminded. He said that the best way to deal with the problem was indirectly, by improving ways to identify feeblemindedness and then committing prostitutes to institutions when they had "socially dangerous tendencies". [126]

A case history that Dummer shared with White altered his opinion about promiscuous women. She told him about a woman who had borne four children, each by a different man. Each time the child was taken by some charitable group and the girl was started again at some

---

125   Dummer Collection #375
126   Dummer Collection #850

work. Each time she repeated the process until she was the despair of the social worker:

> A little flat was rented, her children gathered together from the various agencies and she was put in charge. She fulfilled her maternal impulses; she cleaned the flat; she cooked for her children; she washed and clothed them and sent them to school. Later a neighbor who had watched the whole proceeding married her. They joined the church and were established in society. If we could do away with courts and jails how many human beings might come through their difficulties and attain maturity of emotion and behavior!... We have had so little respect for nature, so little understanding. In the old attempt to save a girl's reputation by hiding her baby, we have been wrecking her mentally, by blocking her natural functioning." If she had indeed changed Dr. White's mind, she must have felt she was making progress. [127]

While Ethel continued to expand her circle of contacts, both short and long term financial support of selected professionals became a significant part of her philanthropy. For example, she gave Milton Singer, Professor of Mathematics and Philosophy at the University of Chicago, a "generous" check making possible a type of research on the creative working of the mind that he indicated was being "sadly neglected" by big foundations. [128] She guaranteed a salary of $4,000 a year for five years for the services of Florence Beaman at the Montefiore Special School for Truant Boys in Chicago. [129] Financial support of two other professionals, Professor William I. Thomas and Miriam Van Waters are fruitful examples of her long term assistance to those she hoped would prove to be influential in expanding knowledge and advancing her main fields of interest.

Discouraged with the medical and legal professionals' attitudes about prostitutes, Ethel turned to sociology. She remembered that Sociology Professor Thomas of the University of Chicago had been interested in

127   Dummer Book, p. 108-109
128   Dummer Collection #755
129   Dummer Collection #466; Dummer Book, p. 232

the Chicago Juvenile Court, and had asked Judge Mary Bartelme to speak to a graduate class studying prostitution. Dummer wrote to him requesting his ideas on the subject. Thomas's response to her request seemed to her of profound importance. In discussing it with Jane Addams, the Hull House leader told Dummer "If you can afford Mr. Thomas's research, I believe you are on the trail of something of as great importance as the work of Dr. Healy." [130]

After an exchange of ideas by letter, Thomas came to Chicago in 1920 to discuss work he might do about prostitution under a commission from Dummer. She explained her theory that criminologists were on the wrong track, that what they called feeblemindedness was the result of shock, scorn and condemnation, and that the girls were as "re-educable" as shell-shocked soldiers after the war. She told him that few doctors supported her theory. Thomas showed definite interest. Ethel prepared a preliminary draft of a contract and asked her husband for comments. "That is not a contract", he said. It's a sermon." She sent a "boiled down" version to Thomas, saying "You are correct in assuming that this investigation brought a sense of relief to me. You seemed to sense some points not always understood by social workers. I hope that your data and interpretation will prove my intuition or vision to be true. I seem to be playing with a big picture puzzle; some pieces fit; others do not. "Patience and perseverance will show the right relationships and perspective. It is a privilege to help evolve order out of chaos." [131]

Thomas accepted her offer of a contract giving him $5,000 a year for two years' part-time work to carry out his research. The contract stipulated that it would be a study "primarily to gather and interpret such data as shall lead to less unjust and futile treatment than is at present accorded so-called delinquent women, changing not only public opinion, but especially altering procedure in our courts, jails and hospitals. It is hoped it may also tend towards a better understanding of human relations and indicate marriage standards based scientifically on biology and psychology rather than on a past system of economics." Thomas

---

130   Dummer Book, p. 99
131   Dummer Collection #785

felt it should be a collaborative effort. He would draw from documents he had; Dummer would turn over to him case histories she had studied which would not have come to the attention of physicians.

During 1921 and 1922, she and Thomas corresponded at length, debating and explaining their respective views on the child and personality, such as the lack of harmonious maturing of intellect, emotion and will. They were both engaged in wide reading on related newly emerging subjects. One of Dummer's particular interests was the relationship of the unconscious, intuition, and creative behavior. She described a "peculiar sensitiveness" that members of her family had to the sufferings of others. At long distance, she explained, she had suddenly felt the needs of people, and acting on impulse, had been able to help them. Her family called this "one of Mother's hunches". She must have faith in her hunches when a hypothesis suddenly flashes into her mind, she explained to Thomas, such as the vision that led to the establishment of Dr. Healy and the Institute for Juvenile Research, as well as the hunch about this current interest. "Please be patient with my wrestling with these things", she wrote. "Life, as I see it, is as yet so unfinished. You intellectuals disagree so among yourselves that I (need to) intuitively sniff here and there, choosing my mental food. I should enjoy occasion to test my choice against your criticism."

They corresponded on such topics as habit formation and substituting creative activity for fear and threat to change behavior. Dummer predicted that what they were thinking about with respect to the child and personality would soon precipitate widespread public sentiment. A perennial optimist, she believed that people were about prepared for it. "It will get into the schools, the women's clubs, the girl and boy scouts; psychoanalysis will take that slant; parents will be involved, etc. I think also this is going to be a woman's movement". [132]

The result of Thomas's research was reported in *The Unadjusted Girl, With Cases and Standpoint for Behavior Analysis*, published in 1923 in the Institute of Criminology's Monograph #5. ("Unadjusted" was then a euphemism for "promiscuous" and "vice", words that had more

---

132   Dummer Collection #875

moralistic and punitive implications.) The book's forward by Ethel Sturges Dummer began "Modern psychology is throwing so much light upon human behavior that concerning delinquency one cannot do better than follow the teaching of Spinoza, 'Neither condemn nor ridicule but try to understand'. Such an attitude led to the establishment of the first mental clinic in connection with a court, where Doctor William Healy revealed astonishing facts regarding causes and cures for delinquency; such an attitude led to this sociological study of delinquency." She went on to refer to the World War I study of arrests for venereal disease, and of the government's interest not only in curing the physical disease but also in rehabilitation. Data gathered by the Girl's Protective Bureau of the U. S. Interdepartmental Social Hygiene Board found a basis for research by social workers and other professionals. "One felt about these young prostitutes that mere suppression by force would not reach the root of the matter, that causes and conditions must be studied." [133]

Reactions to the book reflected the diverse opinions Ethel had encountered, particularly among sociologists and lawyers. A review in *Social Service,* issued by the Chicago Council of Social Service Agencies, called the book "the logical development of the modern theory of delinquency: that mental conflict is frequently responsible for misconduct and that cure may be effected by the freeing of blocked emotion." The reviewer described the book as a plea for solving behavior problems by humanitarian and scientific methods in accord with the highest standards of religion and common sense. Sociology Professor Thomas Eliot of Northwestern University concurred and reported using it in his classes. A colleague had quite a different reaction. John H. Wigmore, Dean of Northwestern Law School and former President of the American Institute of Criminal Law and Criminology, claimed that everyone knows of the reckless immorality and lawlessness of younger people aged 18-25. "It is more or less due to the vicious philosophy of life spread by our schools for the last twenty-five years by John Dewey and others, the philosophy which worships self-expression and emphasizes the uncontrolled search for complete experience. Whatever the temporary cause of this behavior may be, it is in special

133   Dummer Collection #240

need of repression." A handwritten comment on this source by Frank Dummer: "Pretty savage".[134]

Dummer's friend Jessie Taft, Director of the Department of Child Study of the Children's Aid Society of Pennsylvania, found Thomas bringing a fresh mind and point of view to bear on the subject. She adds: "It occurred to me that one of your prime motives in asking Mr. Thomas to write the book was to get him interested in Mental Hygiene." Platt's recent article gives yet another reaction. Though sources were given for most documents that were quoted, it is impossible to tell the sources of all research that contributed to Thomas's conclusions. Dummer and her contacts, most of them women, obviously played a significant role in providing the raw data. Sociologist Platt finds evidence that Dummer influenced the report's general ideas. [135]

During her stay in California in 1920, Ethel Dummer came upon the work of Miriam Van Waters, who was having a successful but turbulent career as superintendent of Los Angeles County Juvenile Hall. [136] Van Waters became another major recipient of Dummer's largesse. The two women soon established a mutually supportive relationship that would prove to have an impact on the way girls and young women were treated in the justice system. Dummer provided the funds, contacts and nationwide exposure for Miriams's work. Van Waters provided expertise and a place to test reform-minded ideas. Together they helped broaden exposure to constructive, new ways to help girls and young women in trouble – reforms that were not generally accepted as constructive. Their friendship lasted many years. Speaking at the 1954 memorial service for her friend, Miriam Van Waters shared, "The unique thing about talking with Mrs. Dummer was that she took your idea without controversy, almost without question, lifted it and sent it winging some place. You always went away with something developing, not only within you but in your thoughts." [137]

---

134   Dummer Collection, #789 & $538
135   Dummer Collection #776 & Platt; op cit; p 27
136   *Maternal Justice: Miriam Van Waters and the Female Tradition,* by Estelle B. Freedman, University of Chicago Press, 1996, p. 74
137   *In Memoriam, Ethel Sturges Dummer,* March 7, 1954; family records.

Van Waters was creating a new type of correctional school called El Retiro, a therapeutically-oriented facility for young women delinquents, including prostitutes and unwed mothers. The program filled the girls' minds with interesting ideas and days of activity. Dummer was impressed to learn, for example, that one little girl who had a part in Maeterlinck's play "*The Bluebird*" had gone on to head the dramatics department of a city school system. Of the first two hundred girls at El Retiro, only two had "drifted back to the underworld". On her frequent trips to Los Angeles Ethel spent half a day at the juvenile court. Then she always visited El Retiro, usually staying in The Colony, a group of redwood houses where Miriam lived with two friends: psychologist Dr. Carol Fisher and lawyer Orfa Shontz. [138] Ethel was pleased to find that the practices at the correctional school, based on Van Water's research in psychology and anthropology, were practically identical to many of the play and education activities that caught their daughters' interest in the Dummer home.

The two women soon learned they had much in common. Their religious backgrounds were similar. Miriam's father was a liberal Protestant minister who embodied the Social Gospel movement, which fostered liberal ideas and social service in Protestant churches at the turn of the twentieth century. [139] Ethel's religious upbringing, combining the Episcopal Church with the new, more liberal Protestant church her father attended, had also stressed social service. Her mother's influence fostered a social consciousness that applied maternal values to bringing about social change.

Dummer and Van Waters made a good team. The older philanthropist introduced her protégé to a national community of reformers, including the Chicago-based network that emanated outward from Hull House. [140] The two women shared the same hope for humanity. Their letters reflect their growing relationship - how they influenced and stimulated each other. Van Waters found in Ethel Dummer one who understood and believed in her method and practice. She referred to the association as "touching hands with something of the spirit". Dummer responded:

---

138 Dummer Book, p. 100
139 Freedman op cit., p. 13
140 Ibid. p. 109

"(That) which no laboratory can test is one of the deepest truths of life. Each gives and receives refreshment of soul. You who are in the thick of the fray feel it is a desperate battle; but to one remote as I am from detailed activity, there is no doubt of the outcome." Explaining her declining to write a paper requested by a Dr. Dicky, because she could think of nothing that seemed worthy of a "platform address", Dummer asked her new friend: "Do you suppose this is due to an inferiority complex caused by my never having had a college education?" Unlike Miriam Van Waters, Jane Addams and many Progressive Era reformers with whom she was in increasing contact, Ethel continued to be overly conscious of her lack of a college degree. [141]

In another letter sharing philosophical thoughts, Van Waters writes, "To me the social worker must preeminently be an artist, must really create the things he desires, as his medium is the most wonderful of all the arts - for it is life itself." (Her use of the male personal pronoun reveals that the women's movement was yet to come.) She enclosed a little "creed" of sculptor Rodin that influenced her, about how an artist must be a man of science, of practice. It concludes: "I know well enough what it is to struggle, for the man who seeks to originate is always in opposition to the spirit of his age". Van Waters ends this letter "To have known you, Mrs. Dummer, is to touch hands with something of the spirit, so rare and delicate, so exhilarating that it is in truth a fresh source of joy and courage." [142] The following year she writes "Your gift to me spiritually has been belief in the essential soundness of our position. Intellectually I knew it; emotionally I felt it; but until you came to El Retiro I was working alone." [143]

In the autumn of 1920 Ethel was invited to be on a program about prostitution for a meeting of state health officers in Washington. DC. She declined to speak, agreeing to provide Miriam Van Waters in her stead. But she attended the conference, feeling that an older woman whose life was conservative though her mind reached into the future should stand back of the younger group who were maintaining that unless there was an emotional adjustment of the girls in clinics the

---

141   Dummer Book p. 101
142   Dummer Collection, #818
143   Dummer Collection , #875

physical cure was futile. She was disappointed and frustrated to find herself a minority of one on the committee of health officers to which she was appointed. "No one seemed to grasp the point that a change of mental and emotional attitude was as important as physical cure. I knew that at the San Diego Hospital fifty percent of the women arrested (for prostitution) were not infected (with venereal disease), and learned that such was true of the clinics throughout the country. What did this mean?" [144]

Orfa Shontz wrote Ethel a confidential letter that fall expressing concern about the state of her friend's emotional and physical health. Miriam's work was "killing her", Shontz said. (Several months later, after Ethel urged her to take care of herself, Miriam explained that working under pressure was the only way she could work. "I have to do things with all my might, quickly with a sort of passion. I suppose that is a limitation. (It is) the way nature insists that I work. So please don't worry about me". [145]) Dummer responded to Orfa Shontz's plea by offering Miriam financial assistance starting with an initial grant of $2,000. In 1920 Miriam received a leave from the Civil Service Commission. Dummer and Miriam Van Waters agreed this would permit the latter to conduct a survey of institutions housing approximately 12,000 girls and young women around the country. They decided she would mostly pick and chose from among the best state schools, rather than emphasizing failures. But visits would also show contrasts with some of the repressive institutions. They agreed on an unstated goal for the survey. It would both expose the horrors of punitive methods and proselytize the El Retiro model nationally. [146]

In one letter with a check to support Van Waters' work, Ethel refers to herself as a silent partner. She occasionally suggested ways her friend could more tactfully represent their views, to be more acceptable to their audience. She had noticed some listeners showing antipathy to Miriam's presentations. "Could you put the spiritual side of all this, or rather the spiritual factor in rehabilitation, in terms scientists would recognize?" she asked. As Miriam traveled throughout the country,

---

144   Dummer Book, pp. 103 & 104
145   Dummer Collection, #819
146   Freedman book, p. 110

keeping that suggestion in mind, she reported finding germs of a new day where real scientific analysis and adjustment were occurring, such as the new progressive farm-schools for women offenders in New Jersey. "I feel that much of our service will be best rendered by pointing out these new elements, stressing them, interpreting them, so that harassed superintendents and timid boards of directors may take courage", she wrote her benefactor. [147]

Miriam kept Dummer apprised of her itinerary and how she was being received. Reactions varied enormously. In several stops in New Jersey and one in New York she reported not receiving a single question about California laws and practice, and no sign of interest in El Retiro, though people she met had heard her presentation at a conference. In contrast, interest in her work was intense among people in institutions in Pennsylvania, Maryland and North Carolina. After she spent a day with Dr. Meyer at Johns Hopkins Hospital, she reported that the work at his clinic was the finest she had seen. Yet she found conditions at the Maryland (Correctional) School for Girls, where he was a board member, "terrible beyond words. They use the factory system, and I shall not tell you all the horrors", Miriam tells Dummer. She reported this reaction to Dr. Meyer, but institutional entrenchment being what it was, "he can't help very much". With Ethel's years of experience trying to help bring about change, that was no surprise. Miriam also described meetings with Lathrop, Thomas, Anthony, Taft, and other contacts that Ethel had arranged for her.

The following summer Miriam enthusiastically wrote Ethel about a new project for neurotic, "psychopathic" and "disturbed personality" girls in Los Angeles. There was no place to send them except to the psychopathic ward or to what she referred to as the insane hospitals. However the county psychologist said she could help these girls if a place could be found. Los Angeles County was doing well housing problem adults diagnosed with these conditions in a cottage; but girls who presented a problem of immorality were not eligible. Miriam went on to tell Ethel about a gift of money to construct a "vacation camp" for these girls, who would be under the supervision of a skilled woman

147   Dummer Collection, #819; Dummer Book, p. 125

trained at Juvenile Hall. She also reported happily on the summer school at El Retiro, with classes in physical education, folk dancing, tennis, and more taught by a "delightful girl" from Hull House. A note at the end of this letter: "How interesting that Dr. Meyer and the others, after two years, are beginning to get the idea. Fertilization of the male mind <u>does</u> take time." [148]

An exchange of letters in 1921 gives insight into how these two dedicated women complemented and supplemented each other as they worked together on their mutual cause. The correspondence also depicts their busy lives. The Dr. Kenworthy referred to is Marion E. Kenworthy of New York, whom Dummer had heard give a paper titled "The Mental Hygiene Aspects of Illegitimacy" at the National Conference of Social Work in Milwaukee. It was the kind of scientific work Dummer had been seeking for two years. Some partially paraphrased excerpts from the Dummer-Van Waters correspondence follows:

> - <u>Dummer to Van Waters, September 10th</u>: I am planning to start for Coronado October 26th. Before that I shall run to New York to plan a meeting with Miss Lundberg, Jessie Taft and Dr. Kenworthy to discuss the subject matter for papers on the "So-Called Delinquent Girl". "What group shall we try next?" Shall it be the Institute of Criminal Law and Criminology? They plan to submit your paper to friends of mine on the Journal of Criminal Law and Criminology. ... I am mailing you a reprint of the Kenworthy paper published in Mental Hygiene. She feels that two of her points were omitted, but admits that it is a milder pill more easily swallowed by the average individual.

> <u>Dummer to Van Waters, September 14</u>: "You show a power of turning out work equal to about ten normal people!"

> <u>Van Waters to Dummer, September 19</u>: "Your letters are like bugle calls, not militarism but of the New Order. ... I cannot tell you how much power is released in those to whom you give the benefit of your vision and your belief. It is a real and

---

148   Dummer Collection , #875

tangible thing, dear friend." She is happy that the Dummers will be in California. "It sounds heretical but I think the scientific group (here) needs enlightenment because they are so often separated by so many mufflers and thicknesses from life. .... Our camp for hysterical girls closed successfully for the summer with a record of eight permanent and disordered girls treated and restored."

Van Waters to Dummer, October 31: "It was wise of you to send me here. (She doesn't say where.) Officials of the old, old (correctional) institutions are here, representing the sentiment of thirty years, even of fifty years ago. Contrasted with the ideas of today, one receives the impression of two generations and such changes, such mingling of the old and new! I have been asked to speak on six different occasions. ... Fifty years ago it was all men. ...One bitterly complained of the program. 'Fancy' he said (in substance) 'putting on such things as topics related to women and children! Why next year, I expect we will be compelled to listen to something on obstetrics.' And no doubt he will be.".... I talked today on correctional education and gave them our message and I trust something of the spirit that you have so fostered and encouraged in our American treatment of delinquency. I wonder if you really know how much you have accomplished. ... I trust you are resting and gaining strength." [149]

- Dummer to Van Waters, December 14: "Am I always a dreamer? Do I see what I desire instead of reality?" Referring to an unspecified meeting, Ethel goes on to say that men are accustomed to the political method. They do not recognize that this is a day of new understanding of human behavior and that all must be open-minded. She explains her method: I take pains to find some point of common effort, and then cooperate at that point with an individual who in other areas does not see my point of view at all. "It is easier to give them what I am thinking if we start from common ground. Is this cowardice,

---

149 Dummer Collection

this declining to fight for the very farthest one can see? I do admire your show in your successful contests, and wish I might help you, but I have no understanding of the political pulling and hauling beneath the surface. May God give you victory."
150

It seems clear from the preceding that Ethel Dummer's methods were early examples of problem solving and conflict management strategies that would become so prevalent at the end of the twentieth century.

The following summer Ethel received an enthusiastic report from Miriam. They had found an old home with ten rooms and a garden in the heart of Los Angeles that they planned to turn into a home for El Retiro graduates. It would be a boarding club for girls who are learning to be self-supporting, she explains. The new field secretary would live there; one girl would be the homemaker with a salary paid by the other girls. It would also serve as a clubhouse for other El Retiro graduates, a place to receive friends and have dancing parties. The Los Angeles Women's Business Club planned to use the house as their headquarters, the girls serving them supper at their monthly meetings. Miriam's theories about rejuvenating the lives of girls and young women who had served in the correctional system were taking hold, with the support of some forward-looking Los Angeles women.

In the spring of 1922, when Miriam's survey was completed, an illustrated article titled "Where Girls Go Right: Some Dynamic Aspects of State Correctional Schools for Girls and Young Women" appeared in a special supplement to *The Survey*. Dummer added an order of five thousand reprints to the publication's regular subscription list, and circulated them widely. They generated interest among a much larger circle than criminologists. For example, The Commonwealth Fund of New York had created a Joint Committee on Methods of Preventing Delinquency. Members included the New York School of Social Work, the American Association of Visiting Teachers (AAVT), and the National Committee for Mental Hygiene. (The AAVT, organized in 1919 at the National Conference of Social Work,

---

150   Dummer Collection, #819

was a national group of social workers working with young children, through the public schools. [151]) Under a five-year grant, representatives of these groups were working together to focus attention on the behavior problems of children. They wrote Dummer requesting 100 copies of Van Waters' article with permission to distribute them freely. [152] "You have discovered a gem in Dr. Van Waters", Julia Lathrop wrote Dummer in a 1923 note. "What you have done to make her known throughout the country is a lovely contribution to us all." [153]

How Best to Handle Delinquency?

Ethel's social work during this period was, as she put it, in *thinking* and in selectively sharing her thoughts. Much of her theorizing was kept to herself while her activities were devoted to circulating mental health pamphlets and providing speakers for conferences. One motive she gives for her wide circulation of papers and pamphlets was that academic minds often failed to recognize the relevance of scientific disciplines other than their own. [154] They were apt to be isolated from each other; so she was doing some cross-fertilizing. But she was not isolating herself from action; her interest in the causes and methods of dealing with delinquency continued.

In the spring of 1921 Dummer had received a letter from E. C. Hayes, President of the American Sociological Society (ASS), asking members to suggest topics for the next annual meeting. (She had been a member of the ASS, based at the University of Chicago, since 1910.) [155] Although the topic she suggested, the need to reform court procedure to secure justice for the unadjusted girl, was not accepted for the general meeting, a research group in the Society agreed to gather data on the subject. That autumn she submitted the following program for the Society's next annual meeting:

- Psychology - The Adolescent Girl, by Jessie Taft

---

151   NOOZ, vol. 3, American Association of Visiting Teachers, Jan. 1935
152   Dummer Collection , #374
153   Dummer Collection , #635
154   Dummer Book, p. 125
155   Women Building Chicago…etc., 1790-1990 , p. 237

- Psychiatry - The Logic of Delinquency, by Dr. Marion E. Kenworthy

- Sociology – Illegitimacy, by Emma O. Lundberg

- Jurisprudence - The Court as Clinic and Methods of Cure, by Miriam Van Waters

Both Jane Addams and Julia Lathrop declined Dummer's invitation to preside at the forthcoming program. Then it occurred to her that after all a grandmother who had raised her own family and was watching the third generation, one who had lived conservatively while her mind reached into the future, could by her presence on the platform sanction the new points of view offered by the young scientific women on the panel. As she boarded the train, Ethel's husband cautioned her: "Remember, a chairman's duty is to introduce the speakers, not to lecture". Acting on his advice, she thought out crisp phrases to introduce each speaker. For Van Waters it was "Justice with the bandage removed from her eyes." [156]

The National Probation Association (NPA) provides another example of how Ethel Sturges Dummer influenced a large organization as a member of its board and as a financial contributor. Excerpts from correspondence reveal how her views on the subject of delinquency only selectively supported the opinions of the head of a large organization. In a letter dated November 23, 1922, Charles L. Chute, NPA's Secretary, calls the work of a committee Dummer headed (not identified) the most important of the organization's activities. After discussing the report to be made at an upcoming conference in Washington, he thanks her for her financial contribution to help publish a paper by Professor Eliot of Northwestern University. He then asks her opinion of the views he expressed in a letter to Eliot, which include his suggestion to emphasize cooperation and a higher standard of work in courts and the schools rather than further discussing controversial questions involved. He also asks Dummer to arrange with Dr. Eliot to present that kind of report in Washington. "If he is planning to emphasize facts in regard to what

---

156   Dummer Book, p. 124

is actually being done with delinquent and pre-delinquent children rather than controversial opinions as to what ought to be done, I believe we will get further. I know that this is also your idea."

Dummer indignantly replied by return mail:

> "What I engaged to pay for was not an expurgated edition of Mr. Eliot's report but the report in full. I saw nothing that needed elimination -- nothing which should antagonize anyone accustomed to thinking. One may not agree with everything one reads but what one is trying to get at is the opinion of the individual who is writing the paper. ... It is for Mr. Eliot, not for me, to accept or reject the changes made in his paper. My purpose would be better served by buying reprints of Mr. Eliot's paper from the Journal of Delinquency than by paying for your printing of a paper that did not carry the strength of Mr. Eliot's opinion. Please consider my financial responsibility in the matter withdrawn until I hear Mr. Eliot's wish."

In an about face, Chute's response is a classic example of trying to pacify an important financial contributor. He tells her that no changes would be made without the author's and her approval, that he agrees with everything she says, that he is for the severest kind of criticism of the failures and deficiencies of probation work, and that adequate and trained personnel is their most important need. He wants the meeting of Dummer's committee in Washington to establish scientific standards for better trained personnel. A 1930 letter from the Association's educational secretary, informing Dummer they are sending 50 copies of the issue of "Probation" containing her article on Mental Hygiene and Religion, adds: "If it is of as much assistance to our 2700 readers as it has been to me in clearing up my thinking on a number of points, I can assure you it will be one of the most valuable articles we have published." They undoubtedly hoped that would mollify her. It apparently did – for awhile.

In 1931 Dummer told Chute she would not be contributing to the NPA that year, preferring to give financial support to organizations that demonstrate better methods rather than those that conduct surveys of old methods. The advance of science, she believed, was proving a point made to him the first day he asked her to join the association, that the schools should prevent delinquency. A May 1932 letter from Law School Dean Justin Miller of Duke University made a plea for Dummer's support. "In view of the difficult financial situation at the present time, I hope…that you may be willing to make a substantial contribution to the work of the National Probation Association". Dummer thanked him for writing fully about his concerns for the Association, saying she could see how his knowledge and wisdom would help bring up standards of probation and prevention of delinquency. "Law schools need more such minds as yours." (In earlier correspondence, Dummer had told Miller his letter was "a veritable tonic" for her in his response and appreciation of her ideas based on the psychology of Mary Boole. It had given her courage to continue trying to get educators to recognize the unconscious mind of the child as Boole interprets it.) Her response thanked Miller for fully sharing his concerns about the NPA and for taking the chairmanship of the committee. Due to the financial depression, however, she must curtail her contributions. "It is always unsolved problems which attract my mind", she told him. But she would continue to supply his committee any material he thought would be valuable for schools and courts.

In May 1933 Dummer wrote Chute:

"When you first asked me to join your association I said I thought the schools should take over this function of adjusting children who were delinquent. You then suggested that I come into the group and tell them so. This I have been trying to do for several years. Meanwhile instead of pressing this side of the problem, you have failed to appreciate it. Because I found better methods of advancing right care and treatment within the school system of a city, I have been devoting my time and energy and funds to constructive experimenting which has so convinced school officials here, that now our superintendent of schools is organizing special conferences on problem cases in his endeavor to keep children from being taken to Juvenile Court."

In May 1934 Chute accepted Dummer's resignation from the Board. His letter reveals more of their continuing differences about the best way to deal with delinquency. He appreciated her wish to devote her energy to changing attitudes in schools and developing competent personnel equipped to deal with causes of delinquency. Then he comments: "I do not think that you can possibly mean it when you say that modern mental hygiene methods of child adjustment should be carried on in schools rather than through courts and probation. Of course these methods must be extended to both and to all other agencies which today deal with children." He reported great progress being made in courts. In Cincinnati, for example, he tells her that over 90% of the complaints that come in from parents, social agencies and attendance officers are socially dealt with by trained and sympathetic workers without any court appearance or court record. [157]

The Family-Changing Ideals of Parenthood 1920-1930

About 1920 Ethel Dummer learned of a psychologist at a Juvenile Court (not identified) who lectured at a state university, who had made the statement "Parents are an unmixed evil." That comment raised Ethel's hackles. Another criticism of the family came from the dean of a large private university, also not further identified, who remarked to her "Marriage is an immoral institution". Dummer asked this dean to write a paper elaborating her thesis, but received no response. Following her usual practice of first studying points of view most opposed to her own, which was belief in marriage and the family, she turned to the Research Group the American Sociological Society (ASS) had formed. A professor in that group remarked: "Well, if the psychologists say the parents are not the people to bring up their own children, let them tell us who are." Under the Research Group's sponsorship, the ASS created a new department on The Family, for which Ethel organized the opening program. It became a very lively group - "another channel

---

157   Dummer Collection , #393, #398, & #399

for the brilliant interpretation of human relations being offered by my new young acquaintances among the scientific women." [158]

Hearing that the ASS would include a roundtable discussion on the family at its next meeting, Hazel Kyrk wrote Dummer that the American Home Economic Association had recently created a committee on Economic and Social Problems related to the Home. She requested information about the program for her mailing list of 150 members. Kyrk, with a PhD degree, was a pioneer in the field of consumer economics. In 1925 she joined the faculties of economics and home economics at the University of Chicago, helping to establish Chicago as a premier university for these subjects. Her courses focused on consumer economics within the framework of the family. [159] With this added announcement, attendance at the Sociological Society's program proved so large that the event had to be moved to a larger auditorium. Due to increased interest, many of the papers were included in the next issue of the *Journal on the Family.*

Following the Sociology Association's panel discussion on the family, Dummer began to receive inquiries and requests to speak on the subject. In a letter to Emma Gunther of Teachers College at Columbia University, Dummer asked, "Is it puzzling to you that a non-professional grandmother who thinks it quite possible to chart some of the rocks upon which homes are breaking should turn her energy into efforts which may prevent human wreckage?" [160] She organized her thoughts from her reading, contacts and experience into a talk, "The Responsibility of the Home" that she gave for a 1921 Conference on Social Hygiene Education, held at a Department of Health meeting in Los Angeles. Advances in psychology are explaining in scientific terms the thoughts of mothers and mystics, she told her audience.

"We all know that actions speak louder than words. But few of us understand the potency of unspoken thought: that thought is never completely dissociated from emotion and its motor

---

158   Dummer Book p. 126
159   *Women Building Chicago . op cit., pp. 483/4;* and *Notable American Women: The Modern Period, op cit p. 403;* Dummer Collection #407
160   Dummer Collection, #407

manifestation; that unspoken thought is potent. The essential home of the child lies in the attitude of the parents toward each other. Jealousy, hypocrisy, antagonism between parents may cause their children mental retardation, physical disease, or delinquency. Mutual understanding, harmony in love, create an atmosphere more important to the development of children than food and raiment."

This has been proven many times in mental clinics and courts. Then Dummer goes on to cite cases from the Chicago Juvenile Court, The Institute for Juvenile Research and the work of psychiatrists Freud, Jung, Adler, Smith and Meyer. Her talk was printed for private circulation.

After her talk, Ethel Dummer was appalled to receive a request to give three lectures on "The Family" at a state university, which she does not identify. She was asked to go further, to give practical advice on the ideal she had offered. She declined, saying that one can offer principles, but that each person must work out the practice for himself. "Like stars, one person different from another in glory". [161] However, her message had appeal for selected audiences. For example, she was asked to talk on the responsibility of the home to the Parent-Teacher Association at Francis Parker School in San Diego. A high school student later wrote about the presentation in the 1922 yearbook. "Mrs. Dummer had made such a scientific study of mental hygiene and its connection with the development of the child ... that her audience persuaded her to conduct a mental hygiene class." The class, including teachers and parents, met each Monday afternoon after school for four months. Ethel Dummer presented papers by foremost authorities, followed by open discussion. "At the close of the class each member felt that it had been of inestimable value." [162]

Under the auspices of the ASS's section on The Family, possibly or probably at Dummer's instigation, the Research Group conducted a large survey of U. S. colleges and universities to help determine the extent of courses on The Family. The Dummer Collection at the

161   Dummer Book, p. 128
162   Archives, Francis Parker School, San Diego.

Schlesinger Library contains three large files on this study including correspondence with professors and descriptions of their courses, from 1926 to 1929.

In March 1923 Ethel wrote Julia Lathrop from Coronado seeking her reaction to an idea that might seem as vague as the work of Dr. Healy had to psychologists fifteen years earlier. Though biologists would not agree, she suggests a study of the mental and emotional attitudes of pregnant women to ascertain if there is a relationship to mental defects in children. Data could be collected by mental hygiene personnel through maternity centers Lathrop was starting. She had found in reading Jacob Boehme, she said, that he shared her belief that mental and emotional attitudes during pregnancy are important to a child's welfare. Yet in a paper by a Dr. Bernard at a Sociological Society meeting, he thought there was no such effect. "You are always so kind to my groupings; does this plan for research in the mental health of pregnancy appeal to you?"

In her reply, Lathrop first commented on reading Dummer's "Responsibility of the Home" -- with a sense of its "sound and sweet inspiration". She suggests that Dummer's words: "Considering that nature has brought us from the amoeba to man, let us take courage" should be placed at the entrance of San Diego's Museum of Man. Though she doesn't know if mental hygiene people in Health Maternity Centers are yet qualified to gather the material Dummer suggested, Lathrop discussed possibilities of pursuing such a study. [163]

Dummer's thoughts increasingly dwelled on the family, but she would not lecture on the subject. She continued her efforts to secure varying points of view from psychologists, psychiatrists, and sociologists, but she did not believe herself ready to offer a "technique" concerning marriage and the family. She had been questioning the methods of child study and parent education that were spreading rapidly. She felt strongly that the fundamentals of the art of living together were as yet too subtle to portray statistically. And she believed that experts, feeling sure of their theories, were teaching dogmatically. So she again "slipped away" from

163   Dummer Collection #636

academic groups to further her private research, which consisted of reading, analyzing, observing, writing notes, reviewing what she had read, and pondering. Thinking about the role of motherhood led her to study the history of marriage and to a further interest in sociology and anthropology.[164]

By 1926 she had apparently pondered enough about parenting that she felt she could write about the subject. In an article titled "Changing Ideals of Parenthood" that appeared in the October edition of *Progressive Education* she showed how much she was influenced by Charles Darwin. He turned us from worshiping our ancestors to reverence for youth, from the god of our fathers to such thought of the Infinite as shall have meaning to our children. Ancient wisdom was based on religion, on a "power above all and in all and through all", she elaborates. Darwin-based modern science is adding to that, "offering biologic memory, a description of that power of response to emergency which has been gradually built up in us on our long journey from the amoeba to man, power not only to adapt to environment but to control it." She refers to behaviors that at some time had survival value for an individual or race as "psychic fossils". We may revert to past behaviors and primitive reactions unless our "energy, libido, élan vital, is meeting reality in some satisfying constructive, creative work, art or social endeavor."

"Progressive parents, whether mechanics or mystics", she goes on to say "must change from primitive fear of unknown forces to faith in the as yet unplumbed power of life. Criticism of parents comes both from courts and clinics." Quoting George K. Platt in "Your Mind and You", she concludes "Mental hygienists are stressing one great point, namely, that in most cases of nervousness, in many cases of insanity, and in almost all cases of child behavior or conduct disorder, the trail leads inevitably and directly back to the home."

Miriam Van Waters is cited in this article as concurring. "Modern society must somehow grasp anew the fundamentals of healthy parenthood. We must help the public to understand the importance

---

164   Dummer Book, pp 130 to 135

of the needs of childhood and a more generous, biologically sound view of family formation", Dummer's quote of Van Waters continues. "We cannot expect youths to be impressed with a shallow concept of the home as a place in which to eat, sleep and receive supplies. It must furnish an emotional background, a sense of warmth and security and a guiding line that can withstand the confused definitions of modern life. This can come about only when adults understand themselves... The desire to do so is the first step." Dummer goes on to describe a recent hypothesis that traces the roots of behavior to the unconscious, and offers an explanation. Emotional development is two-fold: it can explain marital failures and show that in education, developing emotions is equally important to training the intellect. [165]

In June of 1926, Ethel Dummer was informed that she had been unanimously elected as the first Honorary Member of the three-year old American Orthopsychiatry Association. Commenting on her selection, President William Healy expressed the attitude for the entire body, ending in these words from the minutes: "... because she has done so much to further the cause of orthopsychiatry and the interest in and study of the scientific treatment of conduct disorders." The letter from then Secretary-Treasurer Karl Menninger explained the intention of the Association's founders: to centralize the techniques and objectives of psychiatrists, sociologists and social workers primarily concerned with problems of human behavior, particularly anti-social conduct disorders.

During a subsequent trip to her Coronado home to visit her daughter and two San Diego granddaughters, born in 1924 and 1925, Dummer capitalized on her new connection to spread her "magic" in California. She persuaded Dr. Menninger, fast becoming a well-known psychiatrist throughout the country, to speak at a California Conference of Social Workers -- sending him $500 to underwrite the cost. The event was a big success. Dr. Menninger talked to standing room audiences in three morning lectures at the University of California at Berkeley. At his evening lecture in a room nearly twice the size, the audience was lined up three

---

165   Dummer Collection, #243, reprinted from "Progressive Educator, Vol. III #4, Oct./Nov/Dec 1926

deep across the back and down the isles. In addition to social workers, Menninger's talk reached teachers, civic leaders, ministers and many leading physicians. Gratitude to Dummer from those who attended was effusive. From Dr. Giles Porter, Director of the California Department of Public Health: "You cannot possibly realize what you did to set the clock ahead for Mental Health in California by sending Dr. Menninger out. Everywhere that I happened to be during the meetings, his lectures were discussed, and I feel that in spite of all of the many other good things that you have done that this is by far the greatest contribution. I feel that Dr. Menninger almost has the field to himself now."

The Executive Secretary of the California Conference on Social Work told Dummer: "We refuse to let you hide the light of your kindness under a bushel! We must let you know how much we enjoyed Dr. Menninger as the bright particular star on our program and how appreciative we are of your generosity in making it possible for us to have him. ... His name furnished us with splendid pre-conference publicity material and by the time we were ready to open the conference on May 17th, I'm sure everybody far and wide knew that Dr. Menninger was to speak." [166]

Ethel Dummer's reputation as knowledgeable on the subject of the family continued to grow. In 1929 she was invited by Chairman Ray Lyman Wilbur to assist in organizing The White House Conference on Child Health and Protection. As a member of the sub-committee on The Family and Parent Education, she learned that their tasks were (1) to find out what is known about the contribution of the family to the child's health and protection, and (2) to learn where agencies were engaged in desirable parent education practices. Louise Stanley, chairman of the sub-committee, admitted that the latter task was somewhat ambitious. [167]

The Expanding Family and Frank Dummer's Death

By 1924 the Dummers had seven grandchildren, three Abbotts and four Fishers, living in and near Chicago. There were frequent visits

---

166   Dummer Collection , #665
167   Dummer Collection #410

back and forth. Since the Abbotts had no car, Gus would pick them up for visits to the big North Michigan Avenue family home. A purpose of one visit, for example, was to look through costumes collected over the years by the drama-loving family. In one of her many letters to daughter Happy her mother writes: "Katharine took her Scotch suit and the Brunhilde costume and Marion some pearl trim from a party dress." The rest was being packed up to send to Happy's school. [168] The older Dummer daughters were beginning to follow their parents' habit of volunteer activities.

Happy had lived at the Coronado house since she started teaching at Francis Parker School in San Diego in 1918. Another of her loves, the outdoors and horses, led her to buy an interest in a pack-outfit on the eastern side of the Sierras Mountains. In the summer she and her cowboy partner, with their outfit of horses, mules, and cooking equipment took Sierra Club members and other groups on camping trips into the Sierras.

Frances joined Happy at Parker several years later, after graduating from the University of Wisconsin and a summer trip abroad with Mary McDonald. The sisters introduced many activities to the school that they had enjoyed in their youth. Happy loved teaching drama, a central part of the progressive education curriculum. Frances taught arts and crafts, including weaving, a craft she had learned and came to love after visiting Czechoslovakia. Together they established a "Glory Hole", teaching weaving, pottery and metal work to let students' fingers get an early sense of touch. [169]

From 1917 to 1927 Ethel, and Frank as business permitted, spent much of the winter months in their Coronado home. Marion, Katharine and their oldest children frequently joined their parents and, first one and then two, younger sisters for part of these visits. The California sunshine was a welcome relief from the cold, snowy Chicago area. Frank Dummer had ample time there to be close to his grandchildren, to use his early childhood teaching methods with them. A favorite test: as soon as a

---

168   Family correspondence
169   Dummer Book, pp 52-53

grandchild could sit up, he would hand him, or her, a small toy for each hand, then hold out a cookie. He then watched the infant struggle through the challenge of how to get the cookie without relinquishing one of the toys. The three generations enjoyed the sunny weather from the large, sloping lawn with its view of the Hotel del Coronado's small yacht harbor in San Diego Bay; and the Midwesterners shared their love of the ocean, the beach, and exploring tide pools at low tide.

In 1922 Happy Dummer was appointed principal at Parker School. Her mother spent considerable time in Southern California that year. We have seen how she was sharing insights on her favorite topics while visiting with family. She spoke on "The Responsibility of the Home" in Los Angeles, and at weekly meetings with Parker teachers, parents and students, for example.

The following year the Coronado house was the setting for a happy occasion. The family gathered for Happy Dummer's marriage to Murney Mintzer, an Annapolis graduate who retired from the navy shortly after the wedding and became a short story and newspaper editorial writer. The Mintzers built a home two blocks from Parker School in San Diego. From 1924 to 1929 the Mintzers added three girls to the growing number of Dummer grandchildren. Frances returned East, did graduate work at Columbia School of Social Work, and became a social worker for elementary schools in Winnetka, Illinois, living near her sister Katharine.

During winter visits the Dummer parents watched Happy introducing much of the practice upon which she had been brought up, based largely on her parents' theories. One year the kindergarten included several children lacking in motor coordination and unable to relax. She told the teacher she would take the children fifteen minutes each day for dramatic play with music to develop muscular control. As Happy's mother later described the result, their steps and gestures, not consciously described or dictated, came in response to a song or play, with the rhythm of music by a young man playing appropriate melodies on the piano. The children responded, maintaining body-mind unity. In three weeks one mother asked "Is my daughter having anything new? She is a changed child. She has blossomed".

Another innovation Happy introduced at Parker was recruiting an unusual gymnastics teacher. Mr. Tahar, son of an Arabian Sheik and former acrobat and circus performer, had shown remarkable skill in restoring polo players after their accidents. His physical education philosophy, rare in his time, was starting classes with stretches, breathing and bending exercises. He taught tumbling and building pyramids, walking on specially made wooden balls (about 2 feet in diameter), and a slack wire for those with weak ankles. His classes for parents and teachers included exercises for women to ease conditions related to pregnancy and menstruation. Ethel Dummer realized that the group work in forming pyramids made it necessary for students to think of others as well as themselves.

After seeing one of Tahar's classes perform, Miriam Van Waters wrote Dummer, "I am really unable to express my admiration for the work of the Francis Parker School, exhibited in San Diego at the State Conference (of Social Work). The buoyant happiness of the girls, their remarkable cooperation in the most difficult muscular and nervous tasks, the rhythm and joyousness of the whole performance, positively thrilled the spectators. Dr. Fisher visited Parker School and expressed the opinion that had she such a place in Los Angeles to send her problem cases, she would be most hopeful of the outcome." [170]

Letters from her parents to Happy, mostly from her mother, are filled with information about the Chicago area family and about their lives and interests. An excerpt of one from her father in a May 1922 letter to Happy talks about bills he is paying for the Coronado house and getting second keys for the joint safety deposit box for her and Francis. Their father then reports on her mother's travels and busy activities. "After two nights 'ashore', that is in her own bed instead of in a Pullman berth or in a New York hotel room, she is off again today-- not out of town, but keeping appointments, and at conferences or meetings. She asked

---

170   Dummer Book, pp.153-55; *The Francis Parker School Heritage*, Ethel Mintzer Lichtman, page 38; Francis W. Parker School, San Diego, 1985

me to copy for you an extract from a letter received since her return, which I am enclosing."

Much about Ethel Sturges Dummer's life can be found in a voluminous correspondence with her daughter Happy. Because they lived far apart, and because of a shared interest and involvement in education, mother and daughter communicated frequently, sometimes every few days, and at times even more frequently by notes and telegrams. Ethel's letters describe her activities, her thoughts about family relationships, and give insights into her perception of events taking place at the time, as well as her view of what she considered her mission in life. She also talks about visits with Katharine and Marion and their children, and about activities such as going to see an O'Neill play with "Father" and relatives of their generation.

In May 1922 Ethel writes to Happy from Chicago "We rejoice with you over the success of your supervision of the school. I always knew you could do it, but I did not realize the rapidity with which you could bring about changes…. Father and I have settled down quietly here, our occupations being typing and the billiard table." In another letter that year Ethel Dummer responds to questions from Happy about difficulties she is having with the Johnsons and the school. After reassuring the new principal that she could solve the financial and other problems, Dummer adds: "If Father and I can be of any assistance in any (financial) perplexity, you will let us know. It is a bit discouraging to me sometimes that so often my part in life seems the discovery and subsidizing of other people's brains and ability, instead of manifesting my own (family). However if that is my mission in life well and good. Whatever I have in mind or money is at the service of my children."

Ever the feminist and optimist she continues in the letter:

"It does seem to me oftentimes that women have more initiative than men. At least they are far more able in grappling with (a) diversity of problems. I suppose it was because that for so long men in primitive times had to spend all their time in fighting and feasting and the women developed all of the industries and the beginning of agriculture. They seem more constructive. …Happy dear, the kind of school you are making is just the introduction to a better world. As I sit here in my restful greenroom and think about the changes that are coming there is hope in my heart that we shall see the emphasis in life's values pass from property to humanity. You have taught me many things, and you will teach others." [171]

A fall letter to Happy that year reports her mother finding a new outlet for her developing philosophy, a way to enhance and broaden her ideas with her contemporaries. Thirty members of her Women's Club group decided to form a study class. They would meet for lunch every two weeks and discuss changes in social attitudes. They agreed to follow historical and psychological changes in five subject areas: economics, education, religion, politics and morality "to see whither we are tending. Won't it be fun", she writes. "We are all old, only two or three are under fifty, and discussion is to be perfectly free. It will be interesting to find what we are all thinking."

"I am really having a chance to get the new ideas concerning so-called delinquency into the minds of those actually in the institutions", she says later in the letter. She gives as an example that the school superintendent in Lake Geneva, presumably with her guidance, was beginning to understand the "stupidity" of two weeks isolation for delinquent children entering the school system, rather than getting the children back to "normal activity" as quickly as possible. You see I am perfectly hopeless as a correspondent, and as a member of the leisure class. Mother must have been a prophet when she said to me: 'Get thy spindle and thy distaff ready and God will send thee flax.' I thought I could withdraw from the study of delinquency and enjoy the happier work of education, trying out or at least providing the means for you and Frances to try out Father's methods and theories. But day after day some call comes for help and I cannot turn aside this great need.

"Don't let them build a big jail at Coronado as the paper tells is being considered, Confinement doesn't cure. No, do not get into this phase

---

171   Dummer Collection # 167; August 25, 1922 letter to "Dear Happy"

of the game. Stick to the school. It is the way to prevent the failures, and you young folk with new vision are giving us a beautiful world". [172]

A 1928 letter to "Precious Happiness: Father and I are so thrilled over your letter about...you and your conference. (It) just carried us up on the crest of the wave of elation. Bless you all out there, I wish I could ride on the wings of thought and drop in to have a fine old jaw-fest."

After ending the letter with love to the then two Mintzer granddaughters, she adds that in her effort not to get her own satisfaction from drawing children and grandchildren to her, she may seem neglectful. "But if you could hear us talk over our blessed children and grandchildren, our deep satisfaction over your personalities and achievements, you would know that our hearts are with you all always. Your devoted old Mother." [173]

In 1928 the family suffered what was, particularly for Ethel Sturges Dummer, a devastating loss. Frank Dummer became ill in the fall. A stomach problem he had been having was diagnosed as cancer. In a matter of weeks he died.

Progressive Educator 1920-1940

A radical movement, a revolution called "progressive education", was emerging early in the 20th century, created by forward thinking educators and modern scientists of the time. Because it related so directly to her interest in education and how children learn, Ethel Sturges Dummer was swept up in it and became a part of it. She saw it slowly making headway in kindergartens and elementary schools. The term "progressive education" may be unfamiliar to some readers; to those who know it, understanding of the term's meaning varies.

Perhaps the best description of changes can be found in the preface of Lawrence A. Cremin's *The Transformation of the School - Progressivism*

---

172 Dummer Collection October 25
173 Dummer Collection #167

in American Education - 1876-1957. Progressive education began as a humanitarian effort to apply the promise of American life to the new urban-industrial world that came into being in the latter half of the 19th century, he tells us. It was a many-sided effort to use the school to improve the lives of individuals, particularly in urban areas; it had a pervasive impact on public and private schools and colleges. The function of the school was broadened to include concerns for health, vocation, and the quality of family and community life. Reformers applied the results of new scientific research in psychology and social sciences. Instruction was tailored to new kinds and classes of children being brought into the schools in the country's new "universal education". To demonstrate the "spiritual hub" of progressive education, Cremin quotes Jane Addams: "We have learned to say that the good must be extended to all of society before it can be held secure by any one person or any one class; but we have not yet learned to add to that statement, that unless all men and all classes contribute to a good, we cannot even be sure that it is worth having." Because the movement meant different things to different people from the beginning, Cremin concludes, there is no capsule definition of the term "progressive education". His book describes its fragmentation during the 1920's and 1930's and its ultimate collapse after World War II. [174]

A Chicago author in her recently published book *The Progressive Legacy, Chicago's Francis W. Parker School (1901- 2001)*, gives another definition "closer to home" for this account of Dummer's life. "Fundamentally, progressive education was an attempt to change a 5,000-year-old education tradition designed for socially stratified non-democratic societies into a method suitable for educating all of American citizenry for a democracy." [175]

Another term is also associated with the turn-of-the century time. The 1890's was a particularly fruitful era for development in fields of education, social sciences and philosophy, as well as for physics,

---

174   *The Transformation of the School: Progressivism in American Education 1876 – 1857,* by Lawrence A. Cremin; Vintage Books, a Division of Random House, New York, 1964; pp. viii – x
175   *The Progressive Legacy of Chicago's Francis W. Parker School,* Marie Kirchner Stone, p. 14, Peter Lang, New York, etc. 2001

chemistry and biology. After publication of Charles Darwin's *Origin of Species* in 1859, the times came to be identified with the concept of "social Darwinism". Education and mental hygiene were particularly influenced by the birth of a new psychology dedicated to scientific study of human behavior in general and of the mind in particular. [176] Granville Stanley Hall, who earned the first doctorate in psychology at Harvard University, became one of the foremost figures in American psychology and education, influential with teachers and other educators. He concentrated his work on the hitherto unexplored problem of child development. When he became president of Clark University in Massachusetts in 1889, that institution became headquarters of the child study movement, a leading center for research and development in the field. His basic thesis stemmed from Darwin: the development of the individual recapitulates the evolution of the human race.

Several of the most influential thinkers of the time were located in Chicago. The University of Chicago had the first department of sociology in the United States, headed by Albion Small, a spokesman for the scientific study of human behavior. In 1894 the renowned education reformer John Dewey came to the same University to head its department of philosophy, psychology and pedagogy. Col. Francis W. Parker, who had attracted national attention as superintendent of schools in Quincy, Massachusetts, was the principal of Cook County Normal School in Chicago that trained teachers. (He acquired the title of Colonel fighting in the Civil War.) The Normal School later became the University of Chicago's Department of Education. Dewey's son was in a Normal School class taught by Flora Cooke, who later became the principal of the new private school named after Parker. Dewey once referred to Parker as the "father of progressive education".

Parker is often quoted as saying "If I should tell you any secret of my life, it is the intense desire I have to see growth and improvement in human beings --- to see mind and soul grow". His central beliefs were that children learn when they are active, when the activity and the learning have meaning to them, and when their natural impulse toward sociability is integrated into the learning process. When two of

---

176   Ibid, p.100

the Dummer daughters attended the Francis Parker School in Chicago, and one later headed a namesake school in San Diego, the Dummer family obviously became immersed in these educational reforms. Ethel Sturges Dummer and others in the Chicago area working to improve education and the emerging field of sociology could hardly escape the influence of these progressive educators. [177]

Interacting with Leading Thinkers and Scientists on How Children Learn

The Dummers were fascinated in studying the advanced methods of education, trying to apply laws which psychology and efficiency experts were giving the world. Believing that her husband had made a distinct and valuable contribution to the subject, Ethel Sturges Dummer passed on what they were learning. She was pleased at changes slowly making headway in kindergartens and elementary schools. Her own view on the subject is contained in some undated personal notes beginning with the question "What is progressive education?"

The object of traditional education, Ethel Dummer believed, had been to make civilized, disciplined individuals out of young barbarians, and to outfit each of them with knowledge, skills and attitudes to prepare them for life in an individualistic and competitive society. She saw the growth of science and technology leading to competition being replaced by cooperation, the urge for profits by careful planning. (With the vision of hindsight from the beginning of the twenty-first century, many would dispute parts of that prediction.) "The schooling of the future must increase the ability of our boys and girls to stand on their own feet and to decide matters wisely for themselves", she believed, "and it must include an expectancy of change." [178]

The key to progressive education thinking was that the child's mind works when it becomes interested in something. The school provides the tools and opportunity to carry out developing ideas. "Creative energy finds outlet in constructing the useful and the beautiful". In progressive

---

177   Ibid, p. x; and <u>Women Building Chicago – 1790 – 1990</u>, p. 181
178   Dummer Collection, #343

schools this leads naturally to group projects and social consciousness. The new methods were challenging educators. In Illinois Dewey and Parker were encouraging experimentation in different ways in different schools. Some educators were finding that word and number symbols become absorbed unconsciously when based on children's interest. When teachers wrote words and numbers on the blackboard about a class project or an account of a child's home experience, for example, second graders read and more easily understood words and numbers. [179]

Trying to understand as much as she could about what was happening in her fields of interests, Ethel followed her practice of extensive reading, correspondence and other contacts with leading thinkers and practitioners. During the 1920s she gradually perfected her "switchboard" style of philanthropy and influence. In her search for understanding, she continued to seek out, solicit and obtain the help of recognized "experts" who were able to speak with authority on a subject that interested her, in this case educating young children. If the results of her probing were encouraging, if she felt there was value in her findings, she started her campaign to educate parents and professionals concerned about education. The campaign included one or both of her two favored channels for disseminating worthwhile knowledge and experience thus gained. She sometimes organized "conferences", from small dinner meetings and discussions in her home, larger gatherings in dining rooms of clubs or hotels, to seminars or panel discussions to which she invited selected audiences. Secondly, she continued distributing copies of pamphlets, reports or books, and securing permission and circulating reprints of magazine articles. In many cases she assumed the cost of printing and distributing. [180]

For example, in a 1926 letter to Dr. William A. White, Head of St. Elizabeth Hospital in Washington DC, Dummer reveals some of her struggle to apply the thinking of scientists to her emerging views on education. Though she did not understand the pages of mathematical formulae in Lotka's "Elements of Physical Biology" and Guye's "Physio-

---

179   Dummer Book, pp. 264-5
180   Dummer Collection #216, Sketch of ESD by Flora J Cooke, 1944

Chemical Evolution" in her search for answers, she tells White, the philosophic paragraphs were "meat and drink to (her) thirsty mind." She suggested that if George Boole's laws of thought and his understanding of the unconscious mind were applied to education, there would be fewer breakdowns and less strain on the conscious mind, the more recently evolved nerve center. It had suddenly come to her, she said, that her husband's "hobby", that muscular coordination developed mental ability was the clue. [181]

George Boole's widow was another major source of inspiration. Mary Everest Boole had written that all a person takes in through experience with the senses registers somewhere in the brain and becomes material for thought later. (M. E. Boole was having an increasing influence on Dummer's thinking about both education and mental hygiene. Dummer would later have her collected works republished.) Boole sought to integrate progressive educational values into a philosophy that synthesized Darwinian biology and religion. She maintained that organized play encouraged the development of the conscious mind, the means through which the unconscious mind found expression and the basis for social activity. Criminal or antisocial behavior, on the other hand, indicated the continued dominance in adult life of the child's animal or instinctual mind, reflecting a person's neglected education. Dummer believed that Mary Everest Boole best expressed the relationship between impressions through eye, ear, touch, and learning. "By training the hand to trace out Nature's action", Dummer explains in her book, "we train the unconscious brain to act spontaneously in accordance with Natural Law, and the unconscious mind, so trained, is the best teacher of the conscious mind". [182]

Since the 1890s, Frank Dummer had claimed that the school method common at the time hampered the minds of children, and that the mediocrity of humanity was due to inhibitions set up by mother and nurse before a child's 18th month. The most important factor in the education of little children was the coordination of sense and muscle. All forms of motor coordination, he believed, develop the minds of little

---

181   Dummer Collection, #877
182   Dummer Book, pp. 160/61; <u>Notable American Women</u> ....p. 209

children more than the old type of schoolwork. His wife was delighted to find this verified in 1927 by Professor Kurt Koffka of the University of Wisconsin in his book, *The Growth of the Mind,* which said that the weight of the brain gains most just at the time a child is learning to walk. And in 1929 she learned that Professor Kurt Lewin of the University of Berlin, while lecturing at Stanford was saying, "the child thinks with his whole body." To Ethel Dummer, this was the first psychologist whose science agreed with her husband's theories and practices. Progressive education was beginning to recognize the part motor experience plays in the act of learning. Given freedom of motion and objects of interest, a baby studies objects in his environment with touch, taste, smell, hearing and sight. "You can almost see him think." [183]

Another scientist to help awaken and instruct Dummer's interest in the relationship of the brain to early childhood education was Professor Herrick, with whom she carried on a thirty-year association. He was a member of the anatomy department at the University of Chicago, and one of the professors in the first lecture course planned by Dummer in 1910. (That course, titled "The Frontier Line of Science: Questions which Scientists are Trying to Answer" included Herrick's lecture on "The Evolution of Brains".) [184] A 1993 article about Herrick titled "A Humanistic Science: Charles Judson Herrick and the Struggle for Psychobiology at the University of Chicago" refers to him as a "neuroanatomist and psychobiologist". [185]

With a religious background similar to Ethel Dummer's, Herrick believed in applying Christian teaching by working to improve the welfare of the disadvantaged. He shared her growing conviction that social problems had biological roots. He was also dedicated to interdisciplinary collaboration. Grounding psychology in neurophysiology, he saw the capacity of the mind developing as part of organic evolution. Denying the influence of the mind, he argued, was like saying that ideas could not motivate behavior. He believed that successful treatment of delinquency depended on getting delinquents

183 Family Records
184 Dummer Collection , #227
185 Sharon E. Kingsland, in Perspectives on Science, Vol. 1, #3, Fall 1993; University of Chicago Press

to cooperate in their own reform -- that is, be able to control their mental and moral attitudes. [186] Herrick's book *Brains of Rats and Me* showed how the nervous system became thought. "We have now before us", Dummer quotes him, "the anatomical mechanism to record and preserve elements of experience which have been abstracted from many diverse concrete sensory-motor activities, in short, the apparatus of ideation, abstraction, symbolic thinking". [187] What would Dummer and these scientists have thought had they been able to see into the future, how experimentation and new technology at the end of the twentieth century would support some of their theories?

Ethel Dummer began to bring these scientists together to focus attention on the different dimensions of their work, and to provide exposure for them. In 1925 Herrick participated in a symposium convened at the Institute for Juvenile Research to discuss ways of dealing with child delinquency through social science. In a letter thanking him for taking part in the conference, she tells him she continues to believe the mechanism of behavior shows response to emotion rather than reason. "Each day seems an adjustment between our higher nerve center and our spinal column. Whether the life force is a push from within or an attraction from without seems partly a matter of mood". [188]

A typical example of her style is the way she used her honorary membership in the American Orthopsychiatry Association (AOA) and the Illinois Society for Mental Hygiene (ISMH - of which she was a founder) to bring together people from these and other organizations, then spread the results. In 1927, when the role of the unconscious was just becoming the focus of scientific research in several fields, she organized a meeting on this topic under the auspices of the ISMH, inviting scholars she had met through the AOA and other groups as speakers. The gathering included Dr. William White, biologist Charles M. Child, W. I. Thomas, a total of nine professors and other scientists. She then edited, wrote the introduction for, and probably helped finance and distribute copies of the collected lectures in *The*

---

186   Op. cit.
187   Dummer Book, P. 160
188   Dummer Collection #586

Unconscious: A Symposium. It represented the latest research of social psychologists, neurologists, biologists and psychiatrists. [189]

One New York review in *A Review of Better Books* starts out "Anything that Mrs. William Dummer is in gets my humble commendation without delay. So long as I can recall anything about Chicago, she has been putting her support into forward-moving projects." The reviewer refers to her as "modest, quiet, democratic, generous, steady, patient, (and) persistent." The sponsoring ISMH hoped that the seminar would provide "mental hygienists" with the latest experiments and research on the subject of the unconscious. [190]

Another thread of Dummer's thinking led her to ponder some differences she was beginning to see between traditional and progressive education. In the chapter in her book headed "Progressive Education as Prevention of Mental and Social Ills", she sees education divided into two main "channels" which she labels instructional and natural, the former authoritative, the latter experimental. She describes institutional education as handing down fixed knowledge -- training for the ministry, law, medicine, and the profession of teaching. The parallel method is trial and error based on man's natural curiosity, imagination and persistent striving to "better human living", a major thrust of new education methods. She gives examples of two men whose natural tendency clashed with institutional methods: Charles Darwin who wasted his time at the university but became a brilliant and influential scientist, and Thomas Edison, whose teacher told his mother to remove her dunce of a son from school. "Why, during the years when life is largely sensation", she asks, "Do we screw our children into desks five hours a day?" [191]

The Dummers had found educating their daughters that "learning by doing" produced better results than giving or reading instructions. Developments in mental hygiene and education were also showing the importance of creative activities in art, music and literature. And new experience showed how constructive activities in household tasks

189   Dummer Collection , #244; <u>Women Building Chicago...,</u> (etc.) p 236
190   Dummer Collection #244
191   Dummer Book, p. 156

and manual training develop initiative, judgment and responsibility as well as the power to think, she said in "A New Deal in Education", a 1933 radio talk to the Men's Teachers' Union. Basing education on the natural interests of children showed that comprehension comes from experience rather than abstractions. The difference between work and play diminishes in the hands of a good teacher, she added. "During a long life spent in constant contact with little children it has been my experience that the three Rs are almost unconsciously absorbed when secondary to some play interest". [192]

As new experience and research in the fields of sociology and education developed, Dummer saw some overlapping. Her dual interest in mental hygiene and education provoked her to think about which of these fields was best suited to dealing with what features of delinquency and education. For example, she was increasingly interested in the contributions of visiting teachers. In the January 1935 issue of The American Association of Visiting Teachers, she commended them as pioneers who were demonstrating to educators the close relationship between emotion and mental development, showing nursery schools that sensory experiences can awaken a child's mind.

Dummer felt that the intellectual approach to teaching mental hygiene was not being translated into feelings. The book method of the university was inappropriate for young children as it ignored the difference between conscious learning and knowledge absorbed through touch by the nervous system. University students are given statistics and conclusions. She believed that life is an art, and could not be put in rules and regulations. Visiting teachers in schools and other social workers dealing with younger children, she believed, would be in the front ranks in troubling times when attitudes were changing about methods and approaches to the whole field of social work. [193]

As we have seen, when Charles Chute first asked Ethel Dummer to become a member of the National Probation Association, she told him she thought that schools should take over the mental hygiene function,

---

192   Dummer Collection #257, Family records
193   Dummer Collection #265; Dummer Book pp. 128-29.

particularly in dealing with the prevention of delinquency. She resigned from the board several years later, explaining that she was devoting her time, energy and funds to constructive experiments within school systems.

A common thread in Dummer's thinking dealt with the relationship between children and adults. She believed the home atmosphere to be the most important factor in a child's life. The Dummers' relationship with their daughters certainly underscores this. "Children are given manners instead of morals, rules instead of principles and theology instead of religion". "Actions speak louder than words" was a lesson she believed that religious minds had shown for years. Parents complain of lack of respect and reverence, but true respect must be won, not commanded. "Children thrive in an environment of frankness and sympathy", was another maxim she often stated. "Primary education should ever be a testing of things and ideas in order that judgment, rather than obedience be secured". She quotes White as saying that we gather a tremendous number of impressions and a vast amount of information in ways that we are not conscious of. A child who does poorly in school, for example, may come from a family situation loaded with antagonistic emotions. While this was widely understood at the end of the century, it was only an emerging concept in Ethel Dummer's day, with implications for preventing delinquency and changes in public education. [194]

In 1925 a Citizens' Anniversary Committee composed of a number of individuals and societies held a three-day program to commemorate the 25th anniversary of the founding of the first Juvenile Court and the 15th anniversary of the Institute for Juvenile Research. The program described the great contribution of the first child guidance clinic as demonstrating the relation between mental conflict and misconduct, the need to diagnose and treat the cause of behavior rather than merely classifying the offense. Because the psychology of delinquency was so new, the program stated, a symposium on the foundations of behavior from the standpoint of biology, psychology, psychiatry and sociology was included to increase understanding of the inter-

---

194   Dummer Book, pp 128-131

relationship and scientific synthesis. Ethel Sturges Dummer presided at the symposium.[195] Years later Jane Addams commended Dummer for establishing the Institute at the Juvenile Court as "one of the most substantial pieces of work done in that line".[196]

In February 1932, Dr. Adolph Meyer, Psychiatrist-in-Chief at Johns Hopkins Hospital, wrote after sitting next to Dummer at a meeting of colleagues, "I had the feeling of sitting beside the mother of a great movement, with Dr. Healy and his wife, Dr. Bronner, as the first generation of the new dispensation, with the group of adepts they had gathered about them...Some of us have to work rather quietly and in relative isolation. I only want to say that even if not among those figuring at the head of the procession of the loudest propaganda, one is always mindful of these rare spirits that initiate practical progress and have the vision and the helpfulness to make creative evolution evolve." [197]

Chicago Schools: Support & Crisis

While Ethel Sturges Dummer was trying to call educators' attention to how the latest thinking of social and biological scientists related to learning, her attention focused on what was going on in schools. As Program Chairman of the Joint Committee on Education (JCE), she closely followed activities, bringing together people from many civic and women's groups who were interested in creating the best education possible for the city's children. During the 1920's, however, tension was growing between teachers, administrators and decision-makers. By 1920 two-term Chicago mayor William Thompson had turned the Chicago school system into a haven for patronage and graft. When he went too far and became unpopular, he was succeeded in 1923 by Democrat William Dever. One of Dever's first moves was to appoint eight reform-minded people to the school board. The board in turn hired William McAndrew as Superintendent; his priorities included eliminating the dominating influence of politicians and the teachers' unions. McAndrew's tenure, however, was short-lived. In 1927

195   Report by Fiona J. Cooke, Dummer Collection #216
196   Dummer Collection #420
197   Dummer Collection #670

Thompson defeated Dever; the returning mayor again added his cronies to the school board; and McAndrew was terminated a year later.

In 1933 the Board eliminated five million dollars from the annual budget and cut hundreds of teachers. The new Board kept a tight rein on expenses through the 1930's.[198]

The decade of the 1930's, however, held some bright spots for Ethel Sturges Dummer as she continued trying to influence the Chicago schools in what she believed were positive directions. In 1930 Superintendent William Bogan appointed Dummer chair of the new Committee on Progressive Education (CPE), part of his Citizens Advisory Council. She saw this as an opportunity to realize a dream. Her memorial to her husband would not be in stone, but in the effort to introduce his understanding of the learning process of young children into Chicago's schools. Without scientific explanation, she realized that in Frank Dummer's theories and those of Mary Boole lay the why and how of progressive methods. At one of Bogan's luncheons she sat next to a stranger from a university who asked, "What is your interest in education, Mrs. Dummer?" "I am seeking a method of education which does not block thinking", she replied.[199]

As a member of the Joint Committee on Education she had earlier visited a progressive school organized by Dr. J. L. Meriam at the University of Missouri's Department of Education. She had been delighted to find methods similar to those of her husband. Children were learning through experience, not by rote. In March of 1933 Dummer received a latter from Meriam, who was now Professor of Education at the University of California at Los Angeles. He had read in Progressive Education that she was "a public spirited woman …known in Chicago for her active interest in liberalizing education", who now headed Chicago's Progressive Education Committee. He wrote commending her for her leadership. She replied that although Superintendent Bogan was interested in progressive education, with pressure from a group on the Board who knew nothing about education, interested only in

---

198   Dummer Collection #349 – School Situation in Chicago 1930-33
199   Dummer Book p. 127

graft and politics, he was under too much pressure to give attention to changes she and her committee considered necessary. She thanked Meriam for a book list he sent and added "having seen the California schools I realize Chicago lags far behind."[200]

As chair of Bogan's new Parent Education Committee, she arranged a series of talks on education at the Chicago Women's Club, open to public school teachers and principals. Elizabeth Irwin, principal of the Little Red School-House in New York, spoke about the value of excursions (what later became known as field trips) in early grades. Professor Kurt Lewin came to Chicago for three lectures. Miriam Van Waters, author of *Youth in Conflict and Parents On Probation*, described constructive and destructive influences of emotion in the lives of children. Then groups of principals and teachers came together to discuss causes of failure.

During the early 1930's schools and politics continued to be intertwined. Conflicts persisted. When Superintendent William Bogan was a spectator at a meeting of the Illinois Society for Mental Health, he was disheartened to hear many negative comments about a high school experiment that he had authorized. He realized that he risked criticism from the Board of Education, and admitted to some flaws in the project. The audience called him an enemy to progress in mental health. Fortunately, Dr. Singer of the University of Chicago supported the Superintendent's critique as justified by explaining some inaccuracies in the two cases being discussed. Bogan wrote Dummer that if the Board of Education was to support that kind of mental health work, as he hoped, the school system should be prepared to cite cases and use descriptions that would appeal to laymen, particularly women. Board members would not be greatly interested in theoretical advances in mental hygiene, he believed, but might appreciate a strategy to give aid to children and parents in terms they could understand. [201]

In August of 1933, Dummer wrote Superintendent Bogan, appreciating the way he was holding the fort. I still hope something may be brought

---

200   Dummer Book p. 68 – letter from Meriam
201   Dummer Collection #337

into the open "to check the physical wrecking of school buildings", she wrote. She wished politics could somehow be fiscally eliminated from school systems in the city, county and state.[202]

Dummer herself had not commented publicly on this subject. In 1932, however she gave a radio talk that mentioned changes in the real needs of children in public school method, methods used in private schools and taught at the Chicago School of Education for fifteen years. Then in 1933, the September 14th issue of the *Chicago Daily News* included an editorial by Mrs. W.F. Dummer, headed "The School Economy, Wise and Unwise." In some respects when every phase of life seems to be in the process of reconstruction, including the American system of education, Dummer wrote, "we should be careful not to throw out the babies with the bath." She counseled retaining real values and a wise economy, while discarding what was outmoded. She then identified three great Chicago area leaders who had made contributions. Francis W. Parker emphasized the growth of the whole child and that learning comes from interest. John Dewey told us the 'school was for work and not for listening. Then she wrote on the important research of Dr. William Healy in the Juvenile Court that revealed the close relations between mental conflict and misconduct, and showed the cause of behavior lay in the emotional life of the child. She commended their contributions, and added that Professor Thomas D. Eliot of the University of Illinois was among the first to see the relationship of Dr. Healy's work in education.

To her friend Miriam Van Waters she was less subtle. "With our Chicago Schools wrecked by financiers and political gangsters in the Board of Education … it is difficult to describe one's emotion. We must build all over again, but must first educate public school parents."

In the spring of 1929 Dummer and Bogan corresponded about the latitude permitted by teacher Florence Beaman, a graduate of Neva Boyd's Recreation Training School, in her special class of boys with IQs below 65. "I cannot tell you how glad I am for an open-minded superintendent at this time when it is possible to secure Miss Beaman,

202 Dummer Collection #349

and of my appreciation of the fresh atmosphere and attitudes you are introducing into the Chicago school system," Dummer wrote Bogan. He replied that Dummer and Beaman would undoubtedly agree on methods to be used in an experimental class, which Dummer would fund. If the work were confined to the "old time deadly, artificial routine program", he told her, it would be of no value to anyone. Bogan approved her paying Beaman a salary of $4,000 a year for five years for experimental research in treating and educating so-called sub-normal children.[203] Consistent with her style, Ethel Dummer was continuing to have an impact on ways to educate disadvantaged children. Florence Beaman, whose last name became Bock after her marriage, and Dummer carried on a long friendship that lasted until the latter's death. Before her marriage, Beaman had lived for a time in the Dummer's Chicago home, where she became acquainted with members of Ethel's family.

When Beaman offered games and materials instead of busy work to inspire interest, the boys developed the ability to do their own thinking. Reading and arithmetic were given as activities that had meaning, rather than as individual work. "It was fascinating to watch the boys developing the ability to do their own reasoning." Proving Frank Dummer and Mary Boole right, Beaman was reaching the boys through their unconscious. "Becoming interested in something, they lost the timidity of self consciousness and began to function mentally." [204] The key word that expressed the life of the children in Beaman's classes, Dummer said in her report to Bogan, was "spontaneity". Dr. Meyer defined it for the Progressive Education Committee: when a child follows spontaneously an inner interest, a fuller functioning of all his neuro-muscular potential results. The Chicago school system was not the only place in the state trying this kind of reform. About this time education through play was also being carried out at the State School for Feebleminded; and the Illinois State Conference on Public Welfare was attempting to interpret this approach to educating lower IQ children. [205]

---

203   Family records
204   Dummer Book, p. 232; Dummer Collection # 446
205   Dummer Collection # 267

In 1923 the twenty-four story Allerton Hotel was being erected across Huron Street from the Dummers' home on Michigan Avenue, a street that was becoming a busy thoroughfare. The Dummers had been leasing out the street floor of their four-story building to commercial shops, while the family used the upper three floors. As their daughters had married and moved away, they considered moving, but realized that their second floor opened up opportunities for social service. Ethel Dummer turned her private collection of books, magazines and other publications on education and the social sciences into a free lending library and reading room for teachers and principals.[206] The dining room was used for classes, and the large living room for meetings and discussions on educational topics. As Ethel believed that the "breaking of bread" together had sacramental value, afternoon tea and occasional buffet suppers soon turned their home into a place for a widening family circle. The Dummer's second floor was a perfect place for activities of the Progressive Education Committee (PEC).

The first point taken up by members of the PEC was the twenty percent failure repetition in grade 1-B. Principals came together to discuss causes of that failure. They obtained and circulated suggestions from primary teachers. After discussion and with slight alterations, Superintendent Bogan found the committee's recommendations acceptable. He gave them permission to introduce the "activity" method in first grades in certain schools. Ethel Dummer engaged Neva Boyd and Florence Beaman to give a ten-week Saturday morning training class on the activity program for first grade teachers in the Dummer home. Boyd presented the theory of play, followed by practice in games, songs and dances. After lunch, Beaman applied Boyd's theory and practice to the public school classroom.

Beaman's work with teachers had proved effective with first and second grade children who had not yet reached a mental age to learn to read. They were then ready for the regular curriculum by the third grade. Dummer knew that a similar program in the Los Angeles school system was having success postponing teaching reading to all first grade children who had yet to reach a mental age of 76 months. With advice

---

206 Women Building Chicago (etc.), p. 236

of an experienced psychologist, these children were instead given an enriched environment of play and activity. Chicago principal Robert Greg was also having success with a two-year activity program. He and other Chicago principals trying out the program were provided with what Dummer calls a "remarkable" book brought out by the California Department of Education, the *Teacher's Guide to Child Development.* These schools were also provided with large, empty boxes and building blocks to whet students' interest. "The children have all come alive", one principal commented later. [207]

Superintendent Bogan's Advisory Council at first consisted of about 80 citizens of community organizations representing diverse educational interests in Chicago. Groups met with him or his representative to give advice on subjects such as health preservation, juvenile delinquency and character building instruction. The superintendent's immediate staff served as ex-officio members of the Council. [208] The level of community involvement continued to increase under Bogan. The Advisory Council, now made up of Community Council representatives in the 43 districts, grew to over 300 people. Bogan delegated Edward Burchard, who had worked with the Dummers earlier on the Chicago School of Civics project, to be the staff representative. Burchard was responsible for setting up assemblies, for education clubs, and for luncheons with the groups. A July 19, 1930 editorial in the *Chicago Daily News* "When Citizens Aid in Governing" pointed out the value of citizen participation to counter the undue influence of bureaucracies. Individuals and groups should be encouraged to take an active part in the administration of public affairs. Enlightened public officials should welcome such voluntary citizen aid and cooperation, the editor stated. [209] One wonders to what extent members of the school board agreed.

Dummer's correspondence in the early 1930's shows that while some educators and opinion leaders supported changes, others were beginning to turn against progressive education reforms. The following samples from selected sources reveal these trends, and Dummer's perennial optimism and efforts to counter adverse reactions to progressive

207 Dummer Book, pp. 242-244
208 Dummer Collection #337
209 Dummer Collection #338

education. In a letter to Robert Hutchins, President of the University of Chicago, she comments on the distressing results in the philosophy department. She believed that the qualities he and Professor Mortimer Adler had shown would stand them in good stead in meeting vested interests that sooner or later would oppose their theories and practices. She commends him for his strength of will in holding the course to his goal. "You will win", she tells him. [210]

Despite increasing negative pressures, Dummer continued to use her position as chair of the PEC to try to influence policies consistent with her thinking. She wrote Governor Horner of Illinois, urging him to establish a commission to stimulate interest and discussion about the lives of young children to help them in coordinating sense and muscle. She wanted to carry the discussion above local antagonism to a level of "calm intelligent consideration". To show that her interest was not superficial, she enclosed a list of the results of thirteen investigations concerning thought processes and behavior in children in which she had been involved. There is no record of his response.[211]

In a 1932 letter thanking Dummer for a panel discussion of teachers carrying out progressive education methods, an administrative assistant to the Board of Education told her it was pathetic to hear the board members' fear of authority. He pointed out that Superintendent Bogan wished teachers to be given a great deal of freedom, and suggested that she organize a small planning committee to study the circumstances under which the new type of education could proceed more successfully. While Dummer must have been pleased with the suggestion, she pointed out that when the teacher group had voted to carry this matter to the Principal's Club for discussion, the effort had been sidetracked, presumably due to the "serious crises created by the Board of Education". [212]

In 1934 Ethel Dummer suffered an outbreak of an old respiratory problem. One of her sisters said to her: "I think I know what the matter with you is. You are facing something difficult and you are trying to side

---

210   Dummer Collection #598
211   Dummer Collection #259, ESD Letter to Governor Horner
212   Dummer Collection #350 & #351

step it". Saying her sister had "hit the nail on the head", Dummer agreed to consult Mrs. Lippitt, her sister's Christian Science practitioner friend in San Diego. Lending books to teachers and social workers and holding discussions on educational methods had been comparatively simple, she wrote Mrs. Lippitt. But when the Chicago schools became "wrecked" by a political Board of Education and she was asked to serve on committees and write for publications that became a source of conflict. A telegram from Lippitt that suggested readings about science and health brought relief. "Will you continue assistance and instruction" she asked Lippitt, "until I can accept cheerfully the opportunities for service which seem calling to me, or decide definitely which are most important?" [213]

Ethel Dummer continued working with the Chicago schools largely undaunted, her spirits raised by some words of encouragement. Ralph Wetherby, principal of the Thomas School, forwarded to her some testimonials and expressions of appreciation from school people for her interest in public education. He hoped she would find in them a realization of the extent to which her philosophy had permeated the classroom. Included was a letter from a teacher at the Sullivan School in Flossmore, Illinois, saying "in this time of stress, ... I realize I can never repay Mrs. Dummer nor can I even tell her what her friendship for the teachers has meant, but I always remember her in my prayers." [214]

Where is Education Going?

Ethel's attention was not so immersed in the Chicago school system that she curtailed her search elsewhere for knowledge about sources of behavior and how children learn. She continued to test her ideas and insights with leading educators, sociologists and physicians, including those in the emerging field of psychiatry. She was particularly interested in research on the relationship of the brain to early childhood learning and behavior. After pondering the results of her research, she continued her practice of disseminating the implications of what she had learned.

---

213   Dummer Collection, #642
214   Dummer Collection, #352

She wrote Dr. Franz Alexander, Director of the Institute for Psychoanalysis in Chicago, telling him that his research verified her hypothesis that resulted from pondering upon life and literature. She told him she found it astonishing that meditation can gain insight. In response to her suggestion that he write a paper on "What Is Thought", he replied that the state of knowledge of psychological processes was not yet sufficient to treat more than a few generalizations. In another letter she referred to the stimulating experience dining with him at the Dummer home, discussing their closely related vital interests. Four years later, in returning Mary Boole's book he had just read, he told her he found it remarkable - considering it had been written much earlier. He was amazed at the amount of practical and intuitive knowledge it contained. [215]

In December 1931 Ethel Dummer had the audacity to send a set of the Boole books to Sigmund Freud, hoping he might find them interesting. She saw a relationship between Boole's work on the unconscious, particularly as applied to education, and Freud's work. She compared Boole's work studying the physiology of thought to the recent work of Herrick. Freud suggested she send the books to Dr. Ernest Jones, a colleague. Jones found them of no value, saying that was not what Freud was talking about. But Dummer persisted with the contact. In a later letter to Freud she reported that Dr. Alexander found his work paralleled her interest, and she quoted Dr. White as saying that the structure of the mind, laid down through millions of years, be called the organ of the unconscious. She went on to relate the psychological aspects of George Boole's "Laws of Thought" to that of early religious leaders, and Mary Everest Boole's appreciation of the creative power of thought. [216] The Dummer Collection does not include a reply from Freud.

Dr. Samuel H. Kraines of the University Of Illinois College Of Medicine was a frequent correspondent. In 1933 he wrote thanking Dummer for a booklet subtitled "A Man as a United Whole and As Part of Nature as a United Whole". That was recognized theoretically

---

215   Dummer Collection , #425
216   Dummer Collection, #551

but not lived up to in practice, he told her. The mind is a function of the way elements of the body are integrated, he continued. A child integrates all stimuli to which it has been exposed, incorporating all into his life experiences. The individual child is constantly changing more than adults because of the plasticity of its mind.

After completing training at the Institute for Juvenile Research in 1936, Kraines describes the experience as very enlightening. He gives an example of a boy brought in for stealing who appeared to be a "repressed, uncared-for, mismanaged animal", and how facts of his life helped to explain his behavior. Psychologists and psychiatrists were beginning to understand that crime in children, and often in adults, was not willful and antisocial, but maladjusted behavior. "And all this you had the wisdom to foresee many years ago. But not only that, you have inspired enough of us who now have the desire and the drive, I believe, to carry on."

In what appear to be notes for a class lecture, Kraines refers to Dummer's description of the relationship between mathematical, biological, and religious types of thought. He believes her aim of showing that the latter two are but higher integrations of the mathematical processes. He contrasts her mathematical and logical thought with emotional thinking, and itemizes characteristics of each. In 1937 he wrote from the National Hospital, Queen Square, in London telling her that her spirit and enthusiasm are "the force of life, going on, in, and around, all obstacles." He always carries with him her energy-restoring words: "quietly, easily, restfully, patiently, serenely, peacefully, and cheerfully." [217]

Kraines was not alone in acknowledging Dummer's contributions. In 1934, on the occasion of the 25th Anniversary of the founding of the Institution of Juvenile Research, Mrs. William F. Dummer received letters of tribute from twenty-seven scientists, physicians, educators and others who had worked with and/or knew of her. Samples from six of them follow.

---

217   Dummer Collection, #625

Dr. Paul L Schroeder, Director of The Institute For Juvenile Research: The IJR "owes it's existence largely to your insight into the problems of childhood, your initiative and your generosity, and has grown progressively from a service agency of the Dept. of Public Welfare of Juvenile Court of Cooke County, etc... that have come from your devoted service to the welfare of children and through them to all people."

Dr. Isaac A Abt, Pediatrician: "Mrs. Dummer …has been the vitalizing force in the establishment of medical and psychiatric investigations of the children who were brought to the children's court… She has worked quietly and without self acclaim; she has been the effectual force in the growth of mental hygiene in this community." … "Methods employed by the Juvenile Court of Chicago have stimulated interest, not only throughout this country, but also abroad."

William J. Bogan, Superintendent of Chicago Schools: "When celebrating the 25th Anniversary of the founding of the IJR, please emphasize the financial, moral, and inspirational services of that pioneer in educational advance, Mrs. WFD. "The unusual modesty of Mrs. D. has kept these facts from the public. …the work of an educational prophet is not to be taken as a mere matter of course." "In our public schools the service rendered by Mrs. D. has been remarkable. She has brought aid to harassed teachers and hopeless children. Her vision and good judgment have been a constant source of inspiration to me."

Graham Taylor: "She has had the vision of a seer." … "She has the discoverer's instinctive passion for the pursuit of knowledge, in searching to trace and conduct to subconscious origins." She belongs in the first rank of educational pioneers of this quarter century."

William Healy, Judge Baker Guidance Center: "I have admired greatly your unswerving faith in a better destiny for man."

..."You believed in the best application of science to a new field; you believed so strongly that you made it possible to open up that field."

Thomas D. Eliot, Professor of Sociology & Economics, Northwestern University: "Anyone who knows Mrs. Dummer knows that in her presence the meeting of true minds is on the highest level of which one is capable. One feels an immediate stepping-up of ideation and motivation as in an induction coil or transformer; a vivid sense of one's own possibilities previously untapped." ... Mr. and Mrs. Dummer have reached out and universalized their spirit of parenthood "to embrace all disadvantaged children, with the conviction that above all else children need understanding." They are willing "to submit their intuitions and theories and entrust their resources to the test verification by experimental demonstration....The constant brokering of contacts and cross-fertilization of ideas promoted by their favorite devices such as organizing symposia of pioneer thinkers", sending speakers to conferences and printing the results are other examples of their contributions. "Mr. and Mrs. Dummer are themselves an outstanding demonstration of what a home may mean as a power in a community, as an even international influence, which time will cumulate and cannot lose."

That un-attributed one-page tribute is accompanied in the Dummer Collection by the following letter from Ethel Sturges Dummer. "Dear Tom, No one but you could have written that letter. Point by point it just sank into my soul bringing deep satisfaction. Your appreciation of the home Frank and Ethel Dummer tried to create, your keen observation of the various ways and means taken to forward human welfare in different lines, your realizing the harmony of ideals and interests throughout forty wonderful years of living and loving and working and enjoying together, with your knowledge of the homes sprung from our own with their varied   constructive contributions, -- all these phrases so clearly set forth by you, make of your letter a family treasure, an heirloom to be shared by all of our children and grandchildren." [218]

In 1932 Ethel's support of education had taken on another form closer to the needs of her extended family. The Johnsons were divorced and Clara moved to New York. After the stock market crash in 1929, she withdrew her financial support for Francis Parker School in San Diego, and the four high school grades were eliminated. In 1929 teacher Irene Thuli had taken over as principal; Happy Dummer had become Director, giving her more time for her expanding community and civic work. The school struggled on a few years but enrollment had dropped to sixty; parents were working part time in lieu of paying tuition. A few families who could afford it provided scholarships for other students in Parker's "extended family". By 1932 it looked like obstacles could no longer be overcome. Armistead Carter, son-in-law of Dummer's sister Rosalie Sturges Carpenter, had become president of the Parents' Association that oversaw operations. His two step-daughters attended Parker. At a1932 meeting Carter told the Association how Happy Mintzer had sat on the doorstep of a prospective donor all day without eating, the day after announcing to the teachers that their school would have to close that week-end if $3,000 could not be found to pay bills. She got the $3,000, but it did not solve the problem long.

On April 17th Carter reported the desperate situation to Association members. They reluctantly voted to close the school, making the decision official, and the meeting was adjourned. Carter later explained what then occurred: the school was broke; its fairy godmother had withdrawn her financial support, and a world-wide depression was at hand. The Parker Association had little experience and no organization for raising funds to help survive the crisis; progressive education was not fully accepted by the public; and private schools were not very popular in San Diego and the West. After the vote to adjourn, "seeing tears in Mrs. Mintzer's eyes" moved Carter to stand up, call the meeting back to order, and ask for appointment of a committee to try to solve the problem so the school could continue. A committee of five parents, including Carter, Mintzer, and Thuli, got to work with renewed resolve. The Parents' Association

---

218   Dummer Collection #264 & Vol. 4 (oversize)

incorporated to run the school; they filed incorporation papers, and with dedicated work, by the following September Parker School in San Diego had weathered its first storm. [219]

Happy Mintzer's parents in Chicago had kept in close touch with the situation, providing help as their financial situation permitted during January through March, asking how short the school would be each month. In a January letter Happy's mother tells her not to put Mintzer funds in Tal's (Clara's) venture, but save it for themselves. In that letter she goes on "When I do not try to manage the creator's world for him I go on very well. Occasionally I attempt to control the whole world and then I come down suddenly. I must just stick to my school affairs which are coming along astonishingly, notwithstanding unpaid teachers." She reports that her sister Dee (Marian Dauchy) wants to help with funds for the school, and she is sure her sister Rosalie will also help. "Do not worry. I will do whatever is necessary. It will be a fine memorial to the interest in education which has been carried on right through the tribe from Father down to Frances." In an April 26th letter to her sister Katharine, Happy writes, "You just don't know what it did for me to have Mother come out. I feel like a different person. And all the teachers that heard her speak at the school and the parents who heard her at the luncheon have said over and over again how much inspiration they got from her. At first I was afraid that we had asked too much of her, but by the time she went, I really think that she was a bit rested". [220]

The final chapter of Dummer's autobiography, published in 1935, is titled "Integrity". She summarizes what she saw as key points about her husband's views of a young child's learning and those of Mary Boole, linking them with the scientists and other authorities she had heard and read. She contrasts her mother's method of encouraging a child to walk by offering the reward of a piece of candy, with Frank Dummer's method of arranging furniture so a child could pull itself up and easily move from one place to another. His appeal was below the verbal level. Her mother's method, she came to see, encouraged acquisitiveness,

219   *The Francis Parker School Heritage,* Ethel Mintzer Lichtman, Francis Parker School, San Diego, 1985
220   Family files of Ethel Mintzer Lichtman

while the latter emphasized spontaneity; doing rather than acquiring. In another example, rather than use the Arabic symbols for numbers, which don't convey the idea of plurality, she describes how her husband introduced numbers while playing cards and dominoes with young children. Their eyes saw the quantitative pattern while their ears heard the number of the digit shown. [221]

Progressive schools were also emphasizing the group's welfare over wishes of the self. Children were encouraged in elementary grades to overcome self-consciousness by acting in skits and talking, individually and in groups, in front of their class. The "let's pretend" and playing house of little children was carried on by acting in plays and reporting on research and projects at weekly all-school assemblies. A timid child could be "made over" by being a queen or having a key role in a play. When a student is in a play or reads and discusses a poem with the class, human problems and principles register more deeply than when "taught dogmatically to an individual as a pattern for himself and his behavior". Again, morals should be caught, not taught.

Other conclusions about early childhood education that Ethel Dummer reached during her years of study, observation and reading, and her contacts with cutting edge scientists and physicians included:

Spontaneous interest calls forth the fullest neuro-muscular integration of the potentialities of an organism, including a child.

Physical activity, in addition to developing the brain, "stimulates the growth of the extensions of the cells throughout the nervous system ..."

"In all education, there should be less teaching and more learning."

In spite of the resistance of some educators and civic leaders to her efforts to help reform education, Ethel Dummer was pleased with the

---

221   Dummer Book, pp. 269-274

appreciation and recognition she received from others. In 1941 she wrote Herrick about Milton Singer, a graduate student in philosophy at the University of Chicago, who quoted Mary Boole in his thesis and was translating Gratry's "Logique". He had appeared at her library the year before with a copy of Mary Boole's "Laws of Thought" asking if she had that author's "Mathematical Psychology of Gratry and Boole". She lent it to him, suggesting other Boole books. He had returned shortly "with a gentle smile saying 'Mary Boole is the answer to logic'". Dr. Ralph Tyler of the University of Chicago's Department of Education learned of Boole's work through Singer. Tyler and a mathematics professor came to talk with Ethel. At the Dummer dinner table he expressed appreciation of Boole's theory and practice, especially for teaching mathematics to children. She learned later that Tyler had read all four volumes of Mary Boole's Collected Works, and that Singer had introduced Boole in one of his classes. "All that I worked at years ago seems coming to fruition", she told Herrick. [222]

In 1937 Ethel Sturges Dummer had an opportunity to put her knowledge and skills to use to educate a wide audience about issues and the current status of education. Her reading, talking and thinking was making so much progress in her mind, she began thinking about putting together another seminar on education that could become a second volume to "Suggestions of Modern Science Concerning Education". She felt educators were ignoring the message in Dr. While's "Mental Hygiene of Childhood" that emphasized the sequence of growth, letting each ability function according to normal development. She wanted to tie that into Coghill's contribution that the child's responses in early months must be maintained.

Dummer felt fortunate when the seed of an opportunity fell into her lap. In the spring of 1937 Raymond Osborne, who had succeeded Cooke as principal of Francis Parker School, sought her advice about a program for a small group at the Women's Club the following fall to celebrate the 100th anniversary of Col. Parker's birth. She offered to provide the program and immediately set out to line up speakers for a symposium to be part of a larger celebration at the Palmer House. She

---

222   Dummer Collection #587

believed she could attract people who would fit in well with the ideas and methods of Parker, as well as the theories of Frank Dummer and the writings of Mary Everest Boole. It would give progressive educators "the neurological foundation necessary for the integrity of personality, showing mental hygiene to be more than mere emotional adjustment" she wrote her friend Beaman. [223] After her meeting with Osborne, she used her skills and contacts to secure speakers for what became the Francis W. Parker Centennial Conference titled "Where is Education Going?" [224] The October 1937 three-day event was sponsored by Chicago's Francis Parker School and the Progressive Education Association, in cooperation with The Chicago Association of Child Study and Parent Education. The program follows:

Thursday, October 29th – Topic: **The Child as a Whole**; Mrs. W. F. Dummer, presiding, and author of the forward.

1. The Biology of Learning - C. Judson Herrick, *Prof. Emeritus, Department of Anatomy, Chicago University.*

2. The Education of the Whole Child - Robert Morris Ogden, *Prof. Of Education, Cornell University.*

Friday, October 29th – Topic: **The Individual and his Environment**, Dean Ernest O. Melby, presiding.

1. The Child as a Whole and as Part of a Group - Florence Beaman Bock, *The Little Red Schoolhouse in New York City.*

2. Incentive and Penalty in Education - Miriam Van Waters, *Warden of Massachusetts Reformatory for Women.*

3. The Individual and his Environment - Dr. James S. Plant, *Director Essex County Juvenile Clinic, Newark, New Jersey.*

223 Dummer Collection #448
224 Family records

Saturday, October 30th – Topic: **Inter-Personal Relations,** Miss Flora J. Cooke, presiding.

1. The "We" Psychology of Dr. Fritz Kunkel – Ethel Dummer Mintzer, *Director of Francis W. Parker School, San Diego.*

2. Discussion – Led by Perry Dunlap Smith, *Headmaster, North Shore Country Day School.*

In the program's forward, Dummer explains that the selection of the topic "The Child as a Whole" came from her reading Professor George E. Coghill's "Anatomy of the Problems of Behavior". Dr. Coghill, unable to speak himself, suggested Professor Ogden. With Ogden presenting the philosophical and psychological involvement of the child and Herrick elucidating the neurological and embryonic foundation, Dummer predicted, a good discussion was assured.

The second session emphasized the school environment, particularly Professor Charles Child's "Physiological Foundations of Behavior" and his view that "an organism cannot be studied apart from its environment." "The problem of education is to provide opportunity for release of energies and abilities," Dummer continued, "avoiding the repressions all too common in the lives of little children". Miriam Van Waters had become warden of the Reformatory for Women in Massachusetts. Dummer described her "transforming (the) institution into a remarkable educational experiment." Dr. Plant showed how science was advancing understanding of attitudes toward behavior, bringing a new sense of responsibility to the home and school. The topic for the third session dealing with inter-personal relations, Dummer felt, in the past had been "the domain of poetry and religion – a subject needing much research". Presenters were two educators, both graduates of Francis W. Parker School in Chicago.

True to her pattern to disseminate the content of the Parker Centennial program to a wider audience, Dummer underwrote the cost to have it appear the following spring in Northwestern University's *Educational*

Trends. [225] She backed this up by having the talks published in hard-back form, to distribute to her many other contacts.

In the spring of 1940 Dummer received a letter from the President of Northwestern University inviting her to attend their commencement, where she would receive an honorary degree of Doctor of Humane Letters in recognition of her accomplishments in the fields of juvenile welfare and education. In recommending her, the Trustees had acted on the suggestion of the University Senate, composed of senior members of all faculties. Dummer replied that she was somewhat overwhelmed, considering that she had never taught a class or attended college. After the ceremony, she continued supporting child development courses, including one that introduced the work of Swiss psychologist Jean Piaget on children's intellectual growth. Several years later a Northwestern University Course in "Child Development in the Nursery and Primary Schools" was held in the Dummer library. In the announcement, the Director of the University College

Campus in Chicago indicated that the course was available through the generosity of Mrs. William F. Dummer, who contributed a substantial sum for the purchase of films, books and teacher aids, as well as lecturers specializing in the field, and offered her library facilities to students taking the course. [226]

Time for Expanding Family

Despite a busy life with her "professional" interests, Ethel Sturges Dummer continued her close relationships with members of her expanding family. Her youngest daughter Frances, after completing her training at Columbia Teacher College, returned to the Chicago area and became a counselor and social worker in Winnetka Elementary Schools, on Chicago's north shore. So three of Ethel's four daughters now lived nearby. In 1930 Frances married Rae Logan, principal of

---

225 *Educational Trends, A Journal of Research and Interpretation;* April-May 1938, School of Education, Northwestern University.
226 Dummer Collection #276 & #280; *Women Building Chicago ...,* p. 236; Family records

Skokie Junior High. They lived nearby in Skokie, where their son and daughter were born.

Ethel Dummer was gratified as she watched her four daughters' developing interests in addition to being a wife and parent. Each in her own way was following a creed and example set by their parents, volunteering in fields of education, civic and community affairs. Marion volunteered at Chicago's Gadd's Hill Center, a Hyde Park neighborhood club for Polish, German Catholic and Lutheran ethnic immigrants. Katharine continued with the nursery school in the Fisher home for a while. In 1932 one of her mother's newsy letters to Happy told of Katharine's showing her school movies to more than fifty kindergarten teachers with two kindergarten supervisors from the Chicago Normal School. As Katharine's family grew to six children, she became active in the League of Women Voters. The League was founded in Chicago in 1920, the year women finally obtained the right to vote. Katharine would later become an officer in both the Illinois and the National League of Women Voters.

Happy Mintzer moved up to become director of San Diego's Parker School. She now had some time to pursue community service interests, one of Col. Parker's and her school's original aims, as well as the example set by her parents. An article about Mintzer titled "A Progressive Educator", by Irene Thuli who had succeeded her as principle of Parker School, showed how, at the school and in the community, Happy Mintzer carried on one of her mother's traits. "This ability and willingness to understand the other person's point of view and give it respect and attention, even though not agreeing, is fundamental to her personality and is the lodestone which draws so many people to her fireside." [227] Happy's community activities included creating the Civic Affairs Conference (CAF) with Armistead Carter, whose wife was the daughter of Ethel Sturges Dummer's sister Rosalie Sturges Carpenter. The CAF helped elect three apolitical men to the City Council, replacing a mayor and leadership that many San Diegans saw as corrupt. With her sister Katharine's encouragement, Happy organized and served as first president of the San Diego chapter of the League of Women

---

227   Parent-Teacher Courier; May, 1936, p. 14

Voters. She also founded San Diego's Inter-club Legislative Council of women's organizations, and chaired a Citizen's Advisory Committee that led to federally-funded nursery schools for working mothers.

While busy with these civic affairs, Happy found time to create and have produced three sets of wooden blocks she called "Muscular Mathematics for Young and Old – Mathematical blocks which give through eye and hand a foundation for an understanding of Arithmetic, Algebra and Geometry". To honor Mary Everest Boole, the founder of her inspiration, she called them Boole Blocks. Her mother helped her to start marketing them. [228]

Ethel Dummer was not letting the next generation take over. Florence Beaman, whose married name had become Bock, had developed a close relationship with Ethel and her family. In a 1935 note of best wishes to Florence for her expected baby, Ethel proudly reports on the activities of her four daughters. "With all the girls contributing so much I might sit back and loaf, yet even in the old mother, the interest in evolution carries on and I keep busy in the library." (She reports that 1,913 books had been checked out of the Dummer library during the previous three years.) [229]

Ethel Dummer's letters to her family and recollections of surviving grandchildren attest to her strong belief in the importance of family, particularly to close, supportive relationships of parents with young children. That conviction continued with the new generation. By the early 1930's she had fifteen grandchildren. Twelve of them lived nearby during childhood and early adolescence. There were frequent visits with an interested, devoted grandmother. They enjoyed going to her town home on North Michigan Avenue where she now lived on the top two floors with Emma, her housekeeper and cook. She also joined the next two generations on outings nearby, such as helping members of the Fisher family move lumber for a cabin they were building on the Des Plaines River. A surviving Fisher grandson describes a bigger adventure: his grandmother taking him, a younger brother and their

228 Booklet describing blocks, produced in 1931, Family records
229 Dummer Collection #448

cousin Don Abbott on a cross-country motor trip when the boys were about twelve and thirteen, with Gus driving. Heading for California in the open Buick touring car, they made "educational trips" arranged ahead of time, including a visit to a deep underground salt-mine. The responsibility didn't faze her, John Fisher recalls. When food poisoning overcame them, she left them at roadside to obtain medication in the next town. He recalls that one overnight stop provided only an outhouse, an inconvenience their grandmother took in stride.

The three Mintzer daughters saw their grandmother less frequently, during the time she spent in her Coronado home and on visits east. Most summers Happy and her daughters took the three-day train trip to Chicago. It was a treat for the girls sleeping in Pullman berths and eating in the dining car, though at times they had to tolerate the unfamiliar heat and humidity before railroad cars became air-conditioned. Staying with their grandmother in the midst of a big city, with its unfamiliar noises like the Allerton Hotel attendant's frequent whistle for taxi across the street, was another new and exciting experience. They played with games their mother had played with her parents, such as their grandmother's favorite anagrams. There was always a visit to the Orchard, the Dummer's big house in Lake Geneva, where families congregated and cousins enjoyed exploring the woods, helped harvest the hay and put it in the barn, and swam in the lake, just as their mothers had before them. Taking candles as they walked upstairs to bed was a novelty in the old house with no electricity. Surviving grandchildren treasure one picture taken in 1932 on the steps of the Orchard house, showing three generations of the Dummer family – including sons-in-law.

In a July 1937 letter to Florence Beaman Bock, Ethel includes comments about visiting with family members at Lake Geneva that summer, Happy and her three girls and Katharine with her three youngest boys. "I spent five days with them and feel rejuvenated. I go again Monday to stay several weeks. The children are having a grand time." She tells of their riding horseback and swimming, playing tether ball, croquet and other games in the evening. "I am better than I ever thought possible again (after an illness). The Tribe dined with me before the

Logans motored to Montana, and I have a photograph of the fifteen grandchildren together." [230]

In 1938 the Dummers lost another member of their family. Happy Mintzer died of cancer at age 42. The cancer, probably starting in the uterus (before the use of pap smears), had metastasized. Like her mother, Mintzer's interest and influence in education had spread beyond her local responsibilities at her school. At a memorial service in Parker's courtyard, San Diego School Superintendent Will C. Crawford said he had at first been slightly piqued at suggestions he should seek opinions and advice from the director of a private school, but that he had revised his opinion after meeting and talking with Happy. "To all school people, teachers and administrators alike, Mrs. Mintzer has been a sort of unofficial advisor. ... School people have gone to her for advice and counsel. Never has she failed us." Another speaker, representing San Diego women's clubs said that Happy's quick responsiveness and ready sense of humor in all situations made her a vital force drawing all sorts of people to her. She quoted one leader saying "Mrs. Mintzer made us want to do things for her." "Her utter selflessness", the speaker continued, "the habit of stepping aside and giving others credit is familiar to all who knew her."

Ethel Sturges Dummer continued to help fight for the school, to ensure its continuation as Happy had envisioned it, and to ensure that progressive education would continue in San Diego during a vulnerable time. After reading a letter Dummer had written to a Parker teacher, principal Irene Thuli wrote Dummer, "As usual your philosophy is helping us when we all desire to help you. ... More than all else, (Happy's) point of view is our guiding influence. ... She is more alive today than most people who are walking among us." In another letter: "It was so comforting to know how you are accepting this hard parting and starting right in to do what you can to keep Happy's influence alive." In a letter Thuli wrote Dummer after the latter's visit in October: "I can't tell you how grateful we are. Our first month has been a little difficult, as we lacked about $385 of being able to meet our payroll of 62% of original salaries... I can never begin to tell you what it meant

---

to me to have you walk into (school secretary) Mrs. Harrington's office just before our parents' meeting before school began. I have seldom felt so utterly discouraged, and the encouragement that you gave me during the time that you were here has not only helped me but has enabled me to work differently with both the Board and faculty." [231]

Dr. Donald Abbott had died in 1936; his wife Marion and their three daughters moved to San Diego, with the youngest attending Parker. Their son was attending college at the University of Hawaii. In a letter to Ethel Dummer, Irene Thuli told her how helpful it was to have the Mintzer girls staying with the Abbotts while their kitchen was being remodeled, and how much help Marion Abbott was at Parker. She had become an active parent at the school, and soon followed her sister as president of the San Diego League of Women Voters.

Ethel Dummer continued to stay in close touch with Parker School, which was struggling to keep financially sound. Her ties with the school became stronger after her son-in-law Murney Mintzer revealed a fact she had not known. Clara Johnson had told Happy when they announced their engagement that she must remain in San Diego or the school would be forced to close, a decision on which the Mintzers had based their future, which may have partially accounted for Happy's devotion to the school. A 1940 letter Dummer received from Parker Board President George Heyneman pointed out that over twenty-seven years the school's existence had survived as a result of generous contributions by her and members of her family. He thanked her for that, and the $2,000 she had contributed the past year. He told her of the Board's plan to keep expenses at a minimum, to make every attempt to have Parker self-supporting.

On December 31, 1941, it again fell to Ethel Sturges Dummer to be the focal point of the family's rally to "save" San Diego's Francis Parker School. Irene Thuli sent her a copy of her three-page response to a letter she had just received from Clara Johnson, who intended to sell the school. The new board president Edward Hope and several other members of the Board had written Mrs. Johnson in mid-December

---

231   Dummer Collection #799

asking her for her price and terms so they could discuss and determine whether they could buy the school. When Hope had not received a reply, Irene Thuli wrote Clara Johnson that she was greatly surprised to learn from a realtor that he had an exclusive on the property and was showing it to perspective buyers, including a representative of the Catholic church. "I know little about parochial schools", Thuli wrote (with a silent copy to Dummer), "but am of the opinion that that type of education is diametrically opposed to the principles upon which this school was founded. What we have worked for all these years is an un-dogmatic, free environment, where children may develop their finest potentialities and not become tools of any body politic or religion. Because I have put twenty years of love, care and work into the school, I feel free to speak to you frankly about this pending sale." She explained it would take time for the parents' discussion and for faculty to get other positions, but they understood from the realtor "there is no time. If the Bishop closes the deal the school is gone. It is a little difficult to face this situation knowing how many people are closely involved with the building of all Parker School stands for."

Mrs. Thuli went on to remind Mrs. Johnson that the latter had carried the full financial responsibility until 1932; that since then three of Clara's sisters and a niece had contributed generously to keep the school going, and that parents had contributed $7,000 for building three shops. "During the depression teachers got from 49% to 60% of their salaries, working as they never have before or since, with evening and Saturday classes, etc. to make both ends meet. If this had not been the case I am sure the school would have closed and taxes and upkeep piled up here as it has on your home." She reported increased enrolment and improved finances since depression days; new roofs, lighting systems and many other improvements; and parents contributing hours on festivals and dinners to build up funds for the library and scholarships. She ends the letter "I'm sure you will receive this letter in the spirit in which I write it."

Action followed after Ethel Dummer contacted her other Sturges sisters. A January 5th telegram from Clara Johnson assured Irene Thuli she had never intended to sell the school without "affording reasonable opportunity for the continuation through purchase"; and that her oldest son Winthrop (an attorney) would make a trip west in about ten days to discuss any arrangement the Board had worked out at that time. On January 8th Mrs. Thuli reported to Mrs. Dummer there was still no reply to Hope's letter asking Clara to set a price on the school. Other Board members "were astonished – and that is putting it mildly." The trustees reasoned that the price to them would be quite different from an amount Johnson would ask from outsiders, considering their help in upkeep, time and effort, and contributions the Sturges sisters had been making. Additional letters and telegrams followed.

After a two-week visit to San Diego, Winthrop Johnson wrote Mr. Hope on January 28th offering the school property to the parents. "Frankly, when I stepped off the plane", he wrote, "knowing that my mother would have to sell the school, I was not optimistic regarding our hope that the school could be purchased by the Board and continued along present lines. Now, having learned during my short visit a great many things about the school which I did not know before, and having had the pleasure of meeting and talking with the people who are now and for some time have been responsible for the fine record which the school has made, I feel confident that its future is assured." Confirming a telephone conversation he had made several days before, in accordance with his mother's wishes, he offered Parker'sBboard a sixty-day option to purchase the school property for $22,500.

In addition to the Board, Winthrop Johnson had talked to a number of other parents and alumni, and to community leaders with no direct connection to Parker, all of whom felt the school should and would continue. Some gave him money or pledges, which he enclosed. On March 19th Mrs. Thuli thanked Ethel Dummer for her $5,000 contribution and reported over a hundred subscribers to the fund to buy the school, with more coming in daily. She believed it quite possible they would raise the full amount, rather than borrowing, by April 15th, the extended date Clara had given them. [232] At this writing, the two-campus Francis Parker School kept alive by two generations of the Sturges family, remains a top private school in San Diego with

---

232 Dummer Collection

twelve hundred students, kindergarten through high school, looking forward to celebrating its centennial in 2012.

In 1947 Irene Thuli wrote Ethel Dummer saying she couldn't resist the temptation of telling the latter about the impact she had made on education in San Diego. The Assistant Superintendent of the San Diego City Schools, in a talk to Parker faculty, had expressed appreciation of what the school and Mrs. Dummer had given him in developing his philosophy of education. He recalled fifteen years earlier when Dummer spoke to the San Diego City Schools' principals, what she said about unconscious learning and experiences, which provide children the foundation for good learning. He repeatedly referred to Mary Boole, Thuli said, whom he had first heard about through Dummer and Boole's little book on the "Preparation for Science". He also spoke of Happy's fine contribution to San Diego, both in the field of education and civics. In the same letter Mrs. Thuli reported that Mr. Carter had just called after a Rotary Club meeting. The speaker had talked about family life, quoting (Ethel Dummer's) philosophy of education. "He said you had contributed very greatly to the educational thinking in this country." [233] How very gratified Ethel Sturges Dummer must have been to hear about her success in spreading what she had learned about how children learn, through her experience, many contacts, reading and research.

Murney Mintzer and Mrs. Dummer carried on periodic correspondence between her visits to San Diego. In addition to family news, much of it concerned their common interest in San Diego and national news, and in world affairs. After his wife's death, Mintzer tried to do what he could to replace her work with the Civic Affairs Conference and local politics. In March of 1939 he sent his mother-in-law a booklet about San Diego Public Administration to read and share with the Fishers and Logans. He believed it showed that the CAC's work had made a permanent impression on the city and its people. The publication summarized "the fruits of Happy's first community contribution … no less important" he believed, "though such a large part of her share in it was through others and was therefore anonymous." He reported that

---

233   Dummer Collection , #807

many people such as labor groups, antagonistic four years before when the CAC was formed, were now supporters. Though their candidate lost in a recent election but won the next one, he told Dummer, the experience convinced him that "democracy can function successfully and with justice to everyone", with suitable leadership.

A comment in one letter to her son-in-law reveals Ethel Dummer's sense of humor and ability to look at herself objectively. She tells him she is, or has been, a very dominating person, that she is trying to replace this attribute, and curtail interfering, by working on impersonal activities such as abstract ideas. She wrestled with one book sent her to study, another titled *A Critical Period in American History.* It "keeps me out of mischief. Please let your sense of humor see me trying to satisfy a critical sister who thinks I am always boss, and another relative who thinks I should keep to my own domain", probably referring to her giving advice about the Mintzers. "I love you and the children and Happy and think of us all as 'Parts of a Whole'" she tells him.

Most of their letter exchanges at his time regarded the three Mintzer daughters, then age 8 and a half, 13 and 14. In one letter Mintzer describes himself as a "fumbling, often awkward person who is feeling his way into unknown territory". After exchanging letters and undoubtedly phone calls about the following (1939) summer and future education plans for his daughters, he "obeyed an impulse" and went to Chicago for a quick visit with his mother-in-law and sister-in-law. "The entire matter of arranging as well as possible for the future of our three girls seems so much more simple and clear because I have been able to discuss it directly with you and Katharine Fisher", he wrote Mrs. Dummer when he got home. Both of you have garnered so much more wisdom from experience in shaping children's education than I have acquired that it is extremely heartening to feel that I can, when necessary, check my notions against your knowledge." He ends the letter with "I hope the girls are securing moral support (on a canoe trip with the Fishers) which may in some small measure go toward compensating them for the loss of their mother."

Ethel and Frank Dummer's love of camping had carried on in the next two generations. Katharine Dummer and Walter Fisher had gone on a camping trip for their honeymoon. In the summer of 1939 the three Mintzer daughters were introduced to the favorite Fisher family sport of canoeing. They joined the Fisher parents, four Fisher sons and a college friend on a three-week canoe trip in the wilds of Canada, seeing only two people during that time. They were greeted on return to civilization by news of fighting in Europe, what became the beginning of World War II.

Author, Speaker and Philosopher

Though her contacts and correspondence were increasing both locally and nationally, Ethel Sturges Dummer was at first reluctant to speak publicly. Not having any professional training in areas of her developing interests, she was particularly hesitant to talk to professional groups. After her talk on "The Responsibility of the Home" at the Department of Health meeting in Los Angeles in 1921, we have seen how appalled she was to receive a request to give three lectures on "The Family" at a state university. The request to give weekly talks with the "friendly" audience of students, teachers and parents at San Diego's Francis Parker School helped give her confidence. [234]

In speaking to new groups she had to be careful of her terminology. In a talk on "The Duties of Community Agencies Toward the Pre-delinquent" at the Juvenile Division of a Prison Conference meeting in Boston in 1923, she spoke from notes on small slips of paper. Later at home, as she had time, she reorganized her notes trying to re-capture the audience's interest and spontaneous responses. Together with her long habit of writing down reviews of books and her own pondering, her notes became grist for future talks and writing. [235]

By the time she was appointed head of Chicago's Progressive Education Committee she had become competent at organizing her thoughts and experience for speaking. In an August 1932 radio talk for the Men's

234   Dummer Book, p. 128
235   Dummer Book, p. 142

Teachers' Union she titled her topic "The Needs of the Child in the Early Grades". "You don't have to teach (a baby's) eye to see, or ear to hear, or hand to touch" she told her listeners. "Given freedom of motion and objects of interest (the child) will develop rapidly." She described the theories and experience of her husband, the Booles, and Lewin's statement that "the child thinks with his whole body". She then stressed how modern progressive education recognized the implications of creative play, the importance of stimulating initiative and imagination to prepare a child for "real thinking". "Memorizing symbols does not mean understanding, and all too frequently it blocks actual thought" she told the men. [236]

Dummer called another radio talk to the same group the following summer "A New Deal in Education". "It is said that after every attack upon public schools, there has been sudden and rapid advance in our educational system", she began. "The present crisis may prove timely if the interest aroused throughout the city leads us all, parents and teachers, to genuine evaluation of our schools." New developments in the mental hygiene field were showing the importance of expanding progressive measures to the Junior High School, she continued. Where the objects used in instruction, whether in manual training, "household arts" activities, or in art, music and literature are adapted to the state of the youthful mind, "the difference between work and play is minimal, Every task may be converted into play if the task-master be but properly acquainted with his business." [237] Dummer's speaking to this group, whether at their request or hers, shows another avenue she used to influence an important segment of the education community.

Ethel Sturges Dummer was twice urged to write about her life's work. A "leading social worker" asked her to share how she came to her integrated, dynamic philosophy of life; later her daughter Katharine Dummer Fisher said to her "Most people take up philanthropy in a rather hit or miss fashion, but yours has been like a tree, sending down deeper roots each year and having ever widening branches. I wish you would write for us how you came to do what you have done".

---

236   Dummer Collection #253
237   Dummer Collection, #257

These suggestions did not at first bear fruit. When Dummer was in her seventies, however, she began to see a hypothesis which, if true, might be of value to put in writing. So she proceeded to write what she called a "psychological autobiography", a 275-page book, published by Clarke-McElroy Publishing Company in 1935, titled *Why I Think So: the Autobiography of a Hypothesis*. She decided that she wanted to share with young mothers, social workers and teachers of little children the possibilities she saw for a more wholesome approach to life. She describes her reasons for writing the book in the Introduction.

"Bit by bit from personal experience with children and grandchildren, from poetry and philosophy, from the wisdom of various religious literatures, from correspondence and conversation with experts, from the results of research and experimentation, and from meditation both conscious and unconscious were clues which I saw had meaning." She goes on to explain that with each flash of synthesis she had tried to verify with scientific research what was considered her mysticism. For this she needed to take a vast perspective, glimpsing "all Life in Relation to Time". As we have seen, much of her hypothesis was based on the work of George and Mary Everest Boole, on his "Laws of Thought", and on his wife's psychological interpretation and elaboration of her husband's work, after the information on M. E. Boole's book accidentally turned up with her mail. Mary Boole's understanding of the sensory-motor experience as preparation for thinking had come many years before Herrick's laboratory experiments and Frank Dummer's theories about early childhood learning. The connection gave a basis for Dummer's hypothesis.

George Boole had said "In science, there can be no absolutely right impressions; our minds are not big enough to grasp any natural fact as a whole; everything depends on drawing right conclusions from combinations of impressions." Dummer elaborates with words from Mary Boole's "Master Keys of the Science of Notation": "Disappointment awaits anyone who expects to learn from my words. The student must make mind-pictures of the objects themselves, let the impression of them soak through his conscious mind down into his unconscious mind, and rest till God sends the interpretation 'while he sleeps', not all at once, but at successive stages of his mental development; as much, each time, as he is fit to receive." [238]

Had her autobiography been the story of her relationships with the five generations of her "tribe", Dummer tells us, the result would have been quite different. She likens her book to her Road to Xanadu (the idyllic place in Coleridge's poem "Kubla Khan"), which led to her hypothesis concerning education and the prevention of insanity. She compares her self-analysis in tracing the purpose of her life to psychoanalysis. (It was a time when Freud's work in this new field was generating interest, both positive and negative.) In psychoanalysis patients are helped to recall forgotten personal experiences. Dummer traces forgotten ideas from books and other sources in similar ways. It would be interesting to drop a net of personal emotional memories into her unconscious, she says, to get varying traits of personality showing the opposite side of her nature. After reading Groddeck's *The Unknown Self*, "I can find in past behavior selfish egoism masquerading under rationalized kindnesses". But she decided to "let sleeping dogs lie". [239]

Dummer admits that her book's format is unusual; to this and other readers it is confusing in places. Where the author sees logical significance to associations of widely differing ideas, readers can find some of her connections puzzling. She asks our patience if we are to comprehend the type of pondering which seemed to her to bring insight into human situations. Dates of the events she describes are not always clear, nor are sources of her material. One adult member of Dummer's family found the book unreadable when it was published, lacking clarity in the transition between one idea and the next.

Ethel had sent her manuscript to Professor Herrick for his reaction and comments, which she promptly received. He wrote that he enjoyed the opportunity to read it, the enjoyment undoubtedly enhanced by their "warm personal friendship and admiration", and with some "intimate contacts with the long and fruitful program of public service of which (the manuscript) is only a partial record." For the general public, he

---

238   Dummer Book, pp. vii-xi
239   Dummer Book, pp. 218/219

went on, perhaps it would help if the hypothesis whose autobiography is here recorded were clearly formulated at the beginning and the successive steps in its unfolding more sharply delineated.

Dummer's reply thanking Herrick permits insights about her and how she sees her relationship with scholars and professionals. "The book might have been much better had I given much further consideration to revision yet my song seemed to sing itself. I realize the final paragraph of hypothesis may not be clear at first but believe with old Mary Boole that the unconscious mind of the reader will little by little interpret what it has taken in. You academicians use your conscious mind. Most of the rest of us do much of our thinking below the verbal level. I will try however to clarify the development of the idea." [240]

Dummer summarizes her book's theme at the conclusion: "My hypothesis is that to maintain integrity we should remember that the unconscious is the best teacher of the conscious mind of the child; and for a wholesome world we should utilize the ancient levels of the primitive group or social-unconscious found in little children as basic foundations for the development of a fine social consciousness... The individual comes to full development when freed from self-consciousness; the group achieves more when working for an ever enlarging circle." She refers to this as "our common consciousness": the Golden Rule or common sense.[241]

Despite some readers' qualified appreciation of her autobiography, Dummer received considerable praise and recognition. Her friend Helen Baker thanked her for the priceless service "in collecting the wisdom of a beautiful and useful life...It is a privilege to share your adventure in the world of thought". Baker particularly appreciated Dummer's "long view", her thoughts on marriage and divorce, and the thought that (quoting Dummer) "one must grasp whatever truth there is in the idea antagonistic to one's own before being sure of one's position". [242]

---

240   Dummer Collection #586
241   Dummer Book, p. 274
242   Dummer Collection, #270

Dummer received comments about her book in printed reviews written by people who shared her interests and/or worked with her. Though perhaps somewhat biased, collectively they reveal the life, style and personality that account for Ethel Sturges Dummer's inclusion, with much better known women such as Eleanor Roosevelt, Helen Keller, Judy Garland and Grandma Moses, in the Biographical Dictionary *Notable American Women: The Modern Period.*

In one of two reviews Northwestern University sociologist Thomas D. Eliot referred to *Why I Think So* as an account by "one of America's noblest citizens". It showed "the growth and social incarnation of (Dummer's) own mind through some of the outstanding pioneering ventures of mental hygiene and education in the first half of the nineteenth century". Though she always had adequate means to implement her various interests, he points out, she was totally oblivious to this constant in her creative equation. Her ignoring that factor made others feel that her wealth was an accident, not the essence of her achievements. He sees the absence of personal and factual details in her book reflecting her relegation of material things to unimportance – a view that was an integral part of her life. [243]

In another review Eliot writes

"Mrs. Dummer has evinced perennial youth and resilience in her recurrent pursuit of new enthusiasms. That these were not mere tangents, but successive expressions of a continuing faith, may be called a major demonstration of this book. She is quite ready to be called a mystic, but that she calls her faith a *hypothesis* (something under-lying) is significant to her life-long respect for verification. She has put her faith repeatedly to the test of works…Mrs. Dummer has definitely been the Grail Seeker…The higher good, hidden within the present because of the present limits, and accessible through the release of energies when the *limits* of the situation are opened up, enlarged, to include conflicting elements in a larger synthesis - this has always been her goal; and perhaps this is one way of stating the

---

243   Library and Workshop, Social Forces, pp. 584/5

"hypothesis" which she herself never explicitly formulates. To attempt to do so definitively would, of course, crystallize and thereby destroy the very soul of the hypothesis itself: for its growth must and will continue like the chambered nautilus. No figure of speech will hold it for long." [244]

This seems a good explanation of why Ethel Sturges Dummer called her autobiography a "hypothesis".

H. C. Storm reviews Dummer's book in *The Illinois Teacher:*

"Here we have a new book on education by one who has never posed as an educator, a book on the psychology of learning by one who is not a psychologist, but a book on human relations by one who has lived in the thick of things in Chicago for five decades…This wonderful woman, who has been the power behind the throne in so many of the great social and educational reforms in Chicago, this woman whose one great aim has been to make life better and happier for the children and young people of Chicago, this woman of keen brain, broad sympathy and ample material means has been throughout her very busy years, a keen observer of life and an ardent student of sociology and psychology. … Every teacher, every parent and every social worker should read (this book)." [245]

A review by Marian McBee, Executive Secretary of the New York Committee on Mental Hygiene, found Dummer's chapter on "The Chemistry of Humanity" stimulating.

"The effect of personalities on individuals and groups remains an unanalyzed phenomenon, but a real one. Mrs. Dummer herself, although actively and definitely creative, has a far greater effect on people than can be measured in the usual terms of personality influence. She has not only financed studies and researchers, and provided reading rooms and books

---

244   Thomas D. Eliot, Reprinted from <u>American Sociological Review,</u> vol. II, No. 2, April, 1937.

245   H. C. Storm in <u>The Illinois Teacher,</u> June, 1937; Dummer Collection #271

for Chicago teachers, but has stimulated and challenged much real thinking. In addition, in the 'chemistry of humanity' she has been much more than a 'catalytic personality', giving to many people encouragement and inspiration to carry on in the development of the greater social good." [246]

Finally, is an excerpt of Miriam Van Water's review of her friend's book in The Survey Graphic headed "Memories of a Human Soul".

"It is impossible, in this space, to list the contributions of the author to that revolution in public opinion which has changed our treatment of the child delinquent, the unmarried mother, the prostitute, the feebleminded, the truant and backward and insane. In each of these fields she felt the emotion of an awakened social conscience, struggled till she had a workable concept, presented her ideas to 'experts and authorities', stepped into the background, sustained the enterprise, insisted that all credit go to the person, or agency 'in charge'". [247]

Ethel Sturges Dummer must have been thrilled to receive recognition for her book and her literary talents from the Eugene Field Society, a national association of authors and journalists. Despite the fact that some of her writing was of a kind not traditionally recognized in print, a 1938 letter from president John George Hartwig informed her that the Board of Governors had voted her an Honorary Member of the Society. The honor, he informed her, was based on the literary skill and craftsmanship of her book and other published works, and in recognition of her "outstanding contribution to contemporary literature". [248]

---

246 Miriam McBee, Exec. Sec. New York Committee on Mental Hygiene, in <u>The Family</u>, March 1938, Ibid.
247 Dummer Collection #269
248 Dummer Collection, #270, Letter dated Dec. 10, 1938 from John George Hartwig, President, The Eugene Field Society

Self-Publishing

Following her autobiography, Dummer self-published two small booklets that help explain how her thinking evolved in two important areas. Her thoughts about religion were a continuing influence throughout her life. Her autobiography makes frequent reference to her developing spirituality and its relationship to her main fields of interest: education and mental health. But her religious beliefs are difficult to characterize. In *The Evolution of a Biological Faith*, the 38-page booklet she self-published and distributed in 1943, she sets forth more clearly how what she calls her "biological faith" evolved.

Growing up in a large family where love for one another was taught, Ethel had no knowledge of the Westminster catechism "with its fear and hellfire", as she later referred to it. Mary Delafield Sturges brought up her children on the Golden Rule and the Sermon on the Mount, with virtually no theological dogma. Each week Ethel's mother attended the Episcopal Church with her older children. Ethel recalls two early memories that influenced her. As she kneeled on a huge red cushion during the liturgy, the clergyman prayed "We bless Thee for our creation, preservation and all the blessings of this life." The young girl was thankful for her preservation and blessings, but her strong sense of "truth as accuracy" led her to mentally eliminate the word "creation" before saying amen at the end of the prayer. She recalls a curious feeling of resentment that she had been created without her permission being asked. Later she saw this memory as beginning a change of emphasis in her mind from the "outward picture" to a developing "philosophical me". She recalls her mother's suggestion for substitute wording when the congregation kneeled to offer a prayer: "Let the words of my mouth and the meditation of my heart be always acceptable in Thy sight, O Lord, my strength and my Redeemer." [249]

With George Sturges' help, the liberal thinker David Swing, whose background included teaching Greek and Latin, preached in a rented auditorium from 1875 to 1894. His sermons applied the ethics of early cultures as well as of Christianity to problems of the day. Exposure to the

---

249   Dummer Book, p. 5.

combination of these two interpretations of Christianity, which Ethel later attended alternately and heard discussed at the dinner table, were very influential in shaping her spiritual life. She was also influenced by books found on her parents' shelves. It was a joy to discover the 1850 edition of the *Book of Common Prayer* that "gave freedom of worship to all seeking to follow the teachings of Jesus", that "emancipated the forms of worship from unwarranted restrictions of creeds formed by men".[250]

Dummer's evolving faith was influenced by philosophers and religious thinkers of the 1880s who were in turn influenced by Darwin's theory of evolution. One of them, Frances Power Cobbe, had turned from a Christian into atheism, and eventually to a Unitarian faith. Cobbe's psychological analysis of religions throughout mankind, particularly her books *Darwinism in Morals* and *Hopes for the Human Race, Here and Hereafter*, particularly captured Dummer's interest. She cites the following quote from Cobb's essay "The Evolution of the Social Sentiment" as becoming a philosophical foundation stone for her adolescent mind: "The development of social sentiments are not in the earliest stage understood to have any connection with the worship of the unseen powers."

Cobbe believed that all great religions of the East, from Zoroastrianism to Buddhism, had contributed to nourishing "sympathetic affections". She contrasted this with Western organized religion where she saw a "ceaseless effort to shut out inferior and inimical races". Cobbe cites as examples the Catholic Church's thinking it "religiously obligatory to torture the Jew, to slay the Saracen and to burn the heretic", and "the day (not yet a decade ago)" when the United States Supreme Court decreed that "a negro was not a man under the terms of the Constitution". [251]

Forward-thinking people whose works she read, including philosophers, novelists and poets, were caught up in the idea of evolution and its possible impact on society. "The imagination of the intelligentsia

---

250   Dummer Book, pp. 2-6 Evolution of a Biological Faith
251   Ibid, pp. 6-7

poured its religious impulses into social legislation, social evolution, socialism, sociology and social organization", Dummer tells us. She adds in an un-attributed quote: "It takes a generation for an idea to be listened to, a second for it to be understood, and a third for it to be acted upon". [252]

A grandchild had asked her "Do you believe there was a beginning or that there wasn't a beginning?" "Science has not given us an answer yet", she responded. The question recalled her experience when she first became aware of what Hegel called "great moments of becoming" and his combining thesis, antithesis, and synthesis. Her sudden flash of intuition about the integration of subjects in her schoolroom had prepared her for reading thinkers of her time, such as Bergson's "Creative Evolution" and his philosophy of change. Recalling a quotation from The Book Of Common Prayer admonishing readers to "read, mark, listen, and inwardly digest", she was influenced by books of great thinkers like Mark Hopkins and John Fiske, and by Herbert Spencer, who "thought in wholes, and who related parts to the whole". Her booklet on her evolving faith quotes Spencer's comment about the relationship of science and religion in his *First Principals*: "The universality of religious ideas, their independent evolution among different primitive races, and their great vitality, unite in showing that their source must be deep-seated instead of superficial". In his *Outline Study of Man*, Mark Hopkins offered the hypothesis that mind-body was one system; he also authored *Christian Ethics, the Law of Love and Love as a Law*. These thinkers led to Dummer's belief that science and religion had been related throughout decades, somewhat similar to her comment elsewhere that ethics and religion were essentially interchangeable. [253]

In a 1927 letter Dummer had told W. I. Thomas what the term religion meant to her: "the relation of the individual to other individuals and to the whole of life." Lao Tzu and Jesus sensed this relationship, and acting upon it secured results which seemed unnatural", she continued. "Watson (one of the presenters at a Sociological Society meeting) spoke

---

252 Ibid, page 9
253 Ibid., pp. 16-19

in his paper of the Great Therapist. When we understand the interplay of personality, the radiation of personality, we shall have solved the problem of child guidance." [254] As her booklet continues, it begins to clarify what Dummer means by her "biological faith", its connection with the unconscious, with interpersonal relationships, and with the education of young children.

Dummer uses concepts set forth by the Booles and Gratry to illustrate the inner process by which ideas come to consciousness, the *imagination,* an aspect of the *unconscious.* Herbert Spencer said that George Boole made the greatest advance in logic since Aristotle. Mary Boole commented that her husband made every man his own Aristotle, according to his ability. Central ides of George Boole's thinking that particularly influenced Dummer's evolving philosophy include:

> "We cannot deal logically with any statement except by comparing it impartially with the opposite statement."

> "Sound thought is always a pulsation between extremes."

> "In science, there can be no absolutely right impressions; our minds are not big enough to grasp any natural fact as a whole; everything depends upon drawing right conclusions from combinations of impressions."

A key thought had flashed in George Boole's mind when he was a young boy: there are two kinds of knowledge, one from conscious study, the other from an invisible, indefinable source. But Boole never put this early discovery of the "unconscious" into words. [255]

Dummer believed the research of M. E. Boole and Frances Power Cobbe in the 1860s would reach fruition in the twentieth century. She devotes a section on them to give attention to the two "women evolutionists". Their thoughts on the normal and constructive function of the unconscious mind became prominent in her thinking.

---

254   Dummer Collection # 878
255   Ibid., pp. 20-21

With Cobbe's collaboration Boole had written *The Preparation of The Child For Science*, published by the Oxford University Press in 1904. Chapters on The Unconscious Mind and Mathematical Imagination were stimulating parents at England's first Progressive School; they were fascinated watching the sensory development of their infants and children. Boole felt that "the skill of a teacher is shown not by the knowledge she imparts, but by the manner in which she utilizes the *thinking power* of the child." She differentiated between the unconscious mind and the conscious mind, believing the former is the best teacher of the latter—that the completed thought process includes their alternate functioning.

Ethel Dummer credits Freud with first bringing the therapeutic value of the unconscious to the world's attention. Scientists were beginning to recognize that the individual may not be considered except in relation to environment. "Shall we ever discover this chemistry of personality, this influence which seems to permeate humanity?" Dummer asks. In 1919, Dr. William A. White's "The Mental Hygiene of Childhood" had discussed the constructive effect of conscious control of unconscious emotions in parent-child relations. As an example, to Dummer's question, "Can your science tell why the undesirable emotions of adults are so quickly caught by the child?" the psychiatrist had replied "It is as natural as that the milk in the ice-box catches the flavor of onions nearby". [256]

In her autobiography's chapter on Mysticism, Dummer had described a dream or vision she had when she was under medication for an intestinal infection attack. She questioned whether the "dream" was a constructive power of her unconscious, revealing how she saw her relationship with God. She saw herself in a cave by the ocean, like those in La Jolla, California. A ball of golden light drew her on, disappearing and then re-appearing. It occurred to her that she was playing hide and seek with God, and that her family would think her queer if she told them later. When the scene changed to a mesa such as those in La Jolla high above the ocean, "there was exceeding clarity of atmosphere. One is tempted to use the term 'wonderful light', but this would give

---

256 Dummer Book, pp. 28-31

the wrong impression. It was in no way related to sunlight, nor to the 'golden glow' of the old schoolroom experience, but a marvelous clarity, leaving a picture still rather vivid."

Her continuing words describe this important event in her life, what she refers to as her

Mysticism:

> "On a rock was a large woman in gray with a mantle of blue about her. There seemed an unseen presence also. Then followed this dialogue, the words heard within me, but not as if spoken by the woman: 'I have sought the whole world round and have not found Thee. (Meaning God.) Art Thou within me?' The answer came: 'Within thee!' 'Must I to find Thee tear out mine own heart?' 'Nothing else will suffice.' 'Is it *that?*' (Meaning the effort for the juvenile court girls, the unmarried mother.) 'It is on thy path. Thou canst not escape it.'

> This final answer came with the convincing quality which is said to accompany mystic experience. When I came to myself, although I felt weak, there was a strange feeling of peace and assurance that I need not hurry or worry; that whatever I found on my path, whatever came to me to do, would be done by a Power working through me; Matthew Arnold's 'Power, not ourselves, which works for righteousness'".

Dr. White's "Mechanisms of Character Formation" had given Ethel Dummer a scientific understanding of suddenly "seeing clarity" (clairvoyance), the growth and power of attaining higher levels of mental integration through solving conflicts. At times solutions push up from the unconscious. As she recovered from her illness, Dummer felt a sense of peace, that when the time came she would be shown what to do. [257]

---

257 Dummer Book; pp. 74-78

Dummer concludes in *The Evolution Of A Biological Faith* that the essence of religion is a way of life, a following of the Golden Rule, the Law of Love, found in the teaching of Jesus, Lao Tze, and all great "monotheists".

Sociologist Ernest Burgess of the University of Chicago writes:

"(The booklet) is most revealing and stimulating and I find myself in almost complete agreement with all of it. You have done what so few of us have taken the time to do. You have surveyed large areas of human experience and thought and distilled the essences from each into a synthesis, which transcends as it incorporates the different blends. Knowledge is one as the mystics have always realized and as they have ever perceived it. The scientist of necessity fragmentizes it. There must then always be persons like you who have to apply knowledge and therefore demand that the parts be continuously put together as a guide to action. And these parts in separation and isolation too often seem trivial and gain significance and meaning as they are articulated into a larger perspective." [258]

Miriam Van Waters writes from her new job as Superintendent of the Reformatory for Women in Farmington, Massachusetts:

"From the moment I began reading I felt its <u>power</u>…My entire life (for I cannot separate my personal from my professional life) has been and is **a** struggle with the forces expressed in the words 'Idea begets organization, organization destroys idea', yet I do not believe this is inevitable. And in your book you show how the living forces may survive the forms which hold them. I think you do this with great concentration."

Zoologist William E. Ritter at the University of California in Berkeley writes Dummer that both he and his wife were extremely interested in "The Evolution of a Biological Faith". He was so interested that, were he to comment on all of these ideas it would tire her to read such a

---

258   Dummer Collection #278

long letter. He thanks Dummer for referring to him in her booklet as a "zoologist who for years has taught that the brain of man had evolved through the use of the hands".

What Is Thought?

Since the 1920s Dummer had searched for answers to the question "What Is Thought?" In "Mental Conflict and Misconduct" Healy wrote: "Behavior follows Ideation". That led to further questions, such as: did "ideation" include brain and heart, mental process and emotional reaction? At about this time Freud, who was attracting considerable attention, was using the term "unconscious" when referring to hidden neurotic behavior.

When Ethel Sturges Dummer had first become interested in the Juvenile Court children, she had seen Mary Everest Boole's book *The Preparation of the Child for Science*. Its chapters on The Scientific Mind, The Preparation of the Unconscious Mind, the Cultivation of the Mathematical Imagination, and Ethical and Logical Preparation caught her interest. When Frank Dummer read that Boole corroborated his theory, that the most important factor in the development of a little child is the motor coordination of sense and muscle, he sent to London for everything else Boole had written. Before the day of neurological laboratories and Gestalt psychology, Mary Boole was saying that the child thinks with his whole body. Recognizing the important part the unconscious played, Boole claimed that impressions through the eye, ear, and touch registered somewhere in man and became material for thought later. "The analysis is made by projecting the mind outwards, by the observation of outer facts, but the synthesis which completes the sequence take place within." Dummer believes Boole's great contribution was that the completed thought process includes the alternate functioning of the conscious and the unconscious. She compares it to the physical digestion of a cow, chewing the cud in the mouth, alternating with further digestion in the body. Conscious observation or study should sink into the unconscious for further digestion, but ideas from the unconscious must be verified by the conscious, for Boole points out that "imagination taken as hypothesis may be of great value, but taken as fact it could lead to insanity". [259]

Educators had not yet given much attention to this alternating process in human thinking from which, Dummer tells us, "spring the mathematical imagination, the hypothesis of the scientist, the inspiration of the poet and the intuition of the everyday man. To secure the harmonious functioning of the ancient nervous system, (the sensory unconscious) and the new brain of man (the conscious mind), is the problem of education." Boole was finding in England that teachers and parents who understood the relationship between conscious and unconscious "thinking" could be more successful in helping children learn.

Mary Boole's interpretation of the unconscious was very influenced by the "Laws of Thought" her husband had published in 1854, and by two volumes of "Logique", published in 1855 by Alphonse Gratry, a French Catholic scientist. George Boole had held that no conclusion was valid until one had studied sympathetically the point of view most opposed to one's own. After a period of relaxation and meditation, similarities appeared within the differences, offering probabilities. Dummer refers to Dr. White's statement about this experience: "Higher levels of mental integration are attained through the solution of conflict". This truth was also found in the ancient Chinese proverb: "Truth is found through the union of opposites." When George Boole was seventeen, the thought flashed upon him: There are two kinds of knowledge, one from conscious observation and study, the other from some source invisible and indefinable. Mary Boole later claimed that "her husband's flash of insight was synthesis coming to consciousness from past experiences stored in the unconscious."

Gratry also found that there were two kinds of knowledge, the second by far the most powerful and fertile. The first, the syllogistic process of Aristotle, deduces. The other, the dialectic process is argumentative; using material it possesses, it acquires additional fresh material, including negative points of view. Gratry also used a daily time of "silence of the

---

259   "What Is Thought", self published by Ethel Sturges Dummer, 1945; page 4

soul", with pen in hand, which Dummer compares to the process of Yogi. At the end of this time he found that what he wrote had value for the subject he was studying. Mary Boole claimed that the methods of her husband and Gratry gave a perfect skeleton of the mind's normal action. It was clearly a contribution to human psychology. It was a power of human thinking "which seems in times of emergency or conflict to leap ahead to new truth". It is the constructive power of the unconscious, a field needing research, with which Dummer agreed. Boulanger, an eminent engineer a hundred years after George Boole and Gratry, was saying that the most stimulating thing that could happen to a man was suddenly to see value in that to which he had been most opposed. Mary Boole interpreted the thinking of these men as psychological, a natural use of the imagination, altering conscious observation with "non-conscious meditation", followed by later synthesis. In a similar vein, she also called inspiration the correction of error. At the end of the twentieth century some of these features in the thinking process had become central to decision making, problem solving and conflict resolution.

In the logic of Gratry, and in (George) Boole's "Laws of Thought" as scientifically interpreted by Mary Boole, Dummer concludes that the thinking process may be traced in Mathematics, Science and Religion, and that the same laws of thought "hold good" in these three fields. She completes her analysis in this fifteen-page booklet saying that the laws of thought "hold good" in these three fields. The last page of this booklet, titled "Some Queries of Thought", compares features of thinking in the three categories.

Reviews and Articles by Dummer

To spread the theories of Mary Everest Boole, Ethel Sturges Dummer got permission from Boole's literary executors in London to collect her scattered writings and have them re-published in 1931. She wrote the Preface to the four volumes, 1,566-page edition, *Mary Everest Boole - Collected Works,* and helped distribute copies. [260] In 1940 Dummer was asked to write an interpretive review of the Boole collection for

---

260   Dummer Collection, #487

The Beacon, an international magazine for the "esoteric student" with offices in New York and England. Associate Editor Anne Pierce wrote Dummer, "who but you could so well write a review of this stupendous work."

Early the next year Dummer wrote Philosophy Professor Oliver L. Reiser of the University of Pittsburgh saying she had been asked to review his paper "Promise of Scientific Humanism" for The Beacon. She commended him on his brilliant power of analysis and expressed a wish to meet and talk with him. Referring to Alfred Korzybski, whom she had known for years and to whom Reiser had apparently referred, Dummer told Reiser that Korzybski could not understand her simple language describing the psychological interpretation of the non-Aristotelian "Laws of Thought" of 19th century authors George Boole and Gratry in his "Logique". "It must have seemed strange to you", she wrote Reiser, "that an elderly woman who had picked up her education cafeteria fashion at the counter of life" should attempt any comment on your book.

Because of Pierce's special interest in mathematics and intelligence, Dummer wrote her describing an informal supper with a select group of educators, professors and authors. The subject was Mary Everest Boole's "Preparation of the Child for Science" about using the unconscious and conscious mind in educating children. Reiser was the guest speaker. After he had clarified George Boole's mathematical logic through Mary Everest Boole's psychological interpretation, Dummer called on each to comment, based on his or her background. "We were not a committee but a group of inquiring minds." Dummer wrote Pierce that she believed the seeds of thought sown would bring the Booles into current thought, though there had been no "coming to conclusion". [261]

Other reviews Dummer wrote for The Beacon were on *The Philosophy of Science* by Alice Borehard Greene, and on *Levels of Integration in Biological and Social Systems* , with an Introduction by Robert Redfield, which had appeared in volume VIII of Biological Symposia, March,

---

261   Dummer Collection, #706, 707, & 724

1944. Articles she wrote include: "Mary Boole: A Pioneer Student of The Unconscious" in <u>Mental Hygiene</u>, 1931 - which later appeared as a review in 1945, "Mental Hygiene and Religion" in <u>Probation</u>, Vol. 8, No. 6, 1930; "The Philosophy Back of The Five Year Plan" in <u>American Journal of Sociology</u>, Vol. XXXVI, N o. 4, 1933; and "Life In Relation To Time" for the American Orthopsychiatry Association, 1948. Note: A list of Dummer's writing and talks appear in an Appendix.

III. Recognition And Remembrance: 1938-1954

Winding Down

During the late 1930's and early 1940's, Ethel lived on the third floor of the Dummer home with Emma, her "all purpose" helper, continuing to care for her. She was practically a member of the family. The first floor was still rented. The second floor continued to be her lending library, and also contained classroom and meeting space for various activities, used mostly by the Chicago schools. Sigfried and Anna continued to live in their small house behind the Dummer home. Ethel increasingly had to contend with arthritis. As her fingers began to curl, she learned to use her husband's old typewriter. A secretary came three mornings a week to handle her important correspondence, but she still used long-hand for her personal correspondence.

As their children grew, the three remaining Dummer daughters became busier with their various civic activities. Marion Abbott, living in San Diego, became the extended family's connection at Francis Parker School, where her youngest daughter Ruth was in the same class as her cousin Ethel Mintzer. Marion also became active in the League of Women Voters (LWV) there, serving a term as president. Katharine Fisher's primary activity was also with the LWV, where she became president of the Illinois LWV and went on to a position on the National LWV Board. Frances was an active volunteer in the co-op movement.

Ethel continued to correspond with many of her grandchildren as they grew up and moved away from home. She had time to visit with the two oldest Mintzer girls, Katharine and Ethel, who each spent a year living with the Fishers and attending North Shore Country Day School. The headmaster, Perry Dunlap Smith, had been a classmate of their mother at the Francis Parker School in Chicago. The six Fisher children all attended this forward-thinking school. During the war years, as the oldest Fisher sons and Don Abbott became active in various war-related activities, Katharine Fisher put excerpts of their letters in Fisher United News (FUN), which she mimeographed periodically and sent to her family, her mother, and to some of the extended family.

Ethel Dummer financed tuition for her grandchildren who attended college, or to supplement what was needed for those covered by the GI Bill of Rights. In letters to her grandchildren, she would occasionally give them a special gift based on an interest they had shown, or propose a special activity she would fund that might interest them. The suggestion or gift was always followed by her comment such as "please do not feel that Grandmother is forcing this interest (or activity) upon you. It is that I like to open doors of opportunity to you where I can." An example of how closely she followed a grandchild's interests in a 1941 letter to neurologist Judson Herrick thanking him for reprints of three papers in the *Scientific Monthly*, she asks him for a favor for her grandson Don Abbott, whom Herrick had met and knew of his interest in marine biology. Don, a recent graduate of the University of Hawaii, had just been chosen to reorganize some of the University's science courses, to replace a professor who had been called to war service. She asks Herrick to send Don a copy of his articles, which she describes as showing "nature's basis of man's thought processes and mental development" that she thought might interest the young science professor. [262] Another letter shows how Ethel Dummer kept in touch with members of her husband's Dummer family. In a letter to her husband's great-nephew, knowing of his interest in hybrid corn, she sent him an article on the subject from *Science* magazine, instructing him to throw it away if he already knew about it. "It seems rather absurd for an old lady to be subscribing to science magazines but I have

---

262   Dummer Collection #587

been so impressed by recent discoveries that I like to keep in touch with them. ... How I wish I had your scientific mind nearby that I might have time for discussions, getting your point of view." [263] When Frank Logan, her next to youngest grandchild, later attended the University of Chicago, she was pleased to have him nearby so she could talk about mutual interests with at least one of her grandchildren.

On December 16th, 1938, four years after she was recognized at the IJR's 25th Anniversary, Ethel Sturges Dummer again heard words of praise when she attended a Testimonial Dinner in her honor, given by the Chicago Society for Personality Study in recognition of her many services to the development of psychiatry. The following remarks by Dr. William Healy, unable to attend and read at the event, described the beginning of the IJR almost 30 years earlier. "Ethel Sturges Dummer had the rare distinction of not only having instigated enterprises which have made very notable contributions to the advancement of humanitarian science and education but also of being in her own right a highly original thinker", his testimony began. "Indeed, her specific ventures have resulted from her own initiative and logical thought processes... Mrs. Dummer has always been absorbed in the possibilities of the integration of the best thought and best scientific effort that the world has produced." He went on to describe her being far sighted enough to work with him and endow for the first five years the beginnings of what came to be termed the child guidance movement, "so that now there are over five hundred child guidance clinics in this country and many abroad." [264]

By the early 1940's Ethel was beginning to tire more easily. She reported in a letter to a grandchild in July, 1941, "I with I had the energy to open the Orchard or take you on a camping trip the way your grandfather and I took your mother and aunts." In early October the Friends of Mrs. W. F. Dummer received the following note from her three surviving daughters: "So many of our mother's friends have asked us what notice is to be taken of her 75th birthday that we feel they should be given the chance to have a part in its celebration. Both because her friends are

---

263   Family records
264   Dummer Collection. #274

scattered all over the country and because we feel a reception would be too much of a strain for her, we are asking those who care to do so, to greet her by mail." The collection of her records at the Schlesinger Library contains three folders filled with birthday letters she received in response to this note. She must have been cheered reading through these many letters.

"Perhaps few have had so long an association with you ranging back as I can to the School of Civics and early Settlement days", wrote Edward Burchard, "of this long period in which you have given such notable public service to Chicago and done so much for human betterment." He reminds her of the energy she gave to start the School Community Center on its way in Chicago, and the School Community Councils it generated. "Assisting Superintendent Bogan for eight years enabled me to see and appreciate what you were doing for education and the encouragement your work was giving to the better school forces and how much they needed and wanted it". [265] Dr. C. Judson Herrick wrote "The best return we can make to you for your long and productive career of public service is to try to carry on what you have done. In many fields you were the pioneer, and a pioneer you still are." [266]

Dr. Healy wrote from the Judge Baker Guidance Center in Boston, where he had been since leaving the IJR. He tells her that though they have seen little of each other, he has had ever stimulating memories of her belief in an idea. "What started in those three little rooms of the juvenile Detention Home has become a mighty power in the land, - and so largely through your intuition and vision when others were not quite sure." He had given up his practice to start a new idea on its way in the world, he reminds her. But much more than that was "the anchorage to you, through your own attitudes and beliefs, gave for those first fact-finding studies. You and your husband, he with his many practical suggestions, some of which are to be found copied today in almost every guidance clinic." He points to the letterhead of the Judge Baker Guidance Center as, "one small evidence of your idea. Through all your many activities there are many who today will rise up and call

---

265   Dummer Collection #221
266   Dummer Collection #222

you blessed; not the least of whom are indebted to you are those whose activities are concerned with the child guidance movement." [267]

James S. Plant, M.D., Director of the Essex County Juvenile Clinic wrote:

"What does one say on a birthday that just isn't personal at all but rather reaches out into pretty nearly every worthwhile venture in human happiness...in the country? 'Many happy returns' won't do – it has to be something about waves of love and sympathy and understanding that have gone out from you and your home, now coming back carrying new hopes and ventures and faith in the future. You don't need 'thanks' – but maybe on this birthday a little more than on the others, you can feel your own kinship with all people. If there is anything to this friendship with one's unconscious, with one's body, that I know you believe in so deeply – then their must also be this sort of free flow of spirit back from people to you – just as there has always been from you to others." [268]

Educator Flora Cooke's thoughts summarize the accomplishments of her friend and colleague in a five-page letter. "As a mathematician, a woman of 'insatiable curiosity', whose doubts will be satisfied only by proof, you will need reliable statistics to convince you of your unusual usefulness to others." Cooke lists some of her many accomplishments: As a mathematician, a woman of "satiable curiosity, whose doubts will be satisfied only by proof, you will need reliable statistics to convince you of your unusual usefulness to others. ...The panorama which these birthday letters will spread before you ... will show what one purposeful life well directed toward betterment can achieve." Cooke proceeded to enumerate some of the accomplishments of the "purposeful life". Some examples:

In her review of Etherl Sturges Dummer's autobiography for the Chicago Women's Club, "I traced to your door twenty-

---

267   Dummer Collection #222
268   (Ed's note: Not referenced in manuscript)

six notable reforms, no one of which for public recognition is remotely stamped with the 'Dummer' name;

The large number of great experts in their field who have responded to your call to help solve problems. For example: the 1916 conference on science when four great men from Johns Hopkins and the University of Chicago widened the vision of many of us on the relation of biology to education, and the book you published of the discussion that, in my opinion, "deserves a place in every teacher's reference library".

"Your long service to improve theory and practice of public schools – initiated and financed by you, including use of your library as reference for teachers and the many hundreds of discussions by educators around your dinner table."

The number of pamphlets you have published and circulated, all directed toward the goal of better human understanding and securing better opportunities for unadjusted children and adults. This tracing of cause to effect, always with research and efforts to find remedial measures, "to my mind has been remarkably successful". For example, the effort regarding retarded children that resulted in the discovery of a shocking amount of eye strain and malnutrition, the need to establish both physical and mental health, and your insistence that primary teachers wait for "reading readiness".

She reminded Ethel of the time in 1907 when she and her husband had brought their two youngest daughters, who had been schooled at home by their parents and tutors, to Parker School. "We could not foresee what in the years ahead this family would continue to contribute to educational progress, not only to the Parker School but to the country from coast to coast."

She goes on with more examples of this "thrilling and exciting success story, which should be told, not for aggrandizement, but for the inspiration it could give to other lives." [269]

Move to the Fishers

Five years later, Ethel wrote a granddaughter that she was in better health at 80 than she had been at 75. Her arthritis was still bothering her, particularly in her curled fingers and now her knees. She had learned to cope with the fingers handicap; however her knees were becoming so painful going up and down stairs that she had an elevator installed. One day, on Emma's day off, she came face to face with a new challenge. Gus had brought her home after a meeting, leaving her at her front door. As she was walking up the stairs, she encountered an unfamiliar man with a sack over his shoulder coming down. As he was obviously a burglar, she stepped aside to let him pass. When she got to the third floor that she now lived on, and looked for what might be missing, it became clear that the only room disrupted was the dinning room. Gone were the six place settings of her twelve-piece, monogrammed silverware (the other six were safe in the bank), and several other cherished items from the sideboard.

Because both Emma and Anna had been ill, Marion Abbott came from California to stay with her mother for a while. Before she went back to California, the three daughters decided to engage a nurse-companion for their mother. But after a short while, the woman decided that Mrs. Dummer's case did not lead toward advancement in her profession, so she suddenly left. Frances "rescued" her and took her to stay at the Logan home for awhile. When Frances became ill, Katharine Fisher "took charge" and settled her in the Fisher home. In May, 1947, Ethel wrote her granddaughter "I have moved to my permanent home for the future with Katharine and Walter Fisher. ...They have made every plan possible for my comfort giving me two lovely rooms, one for bedroom and living room, the other for a library. They moved my book shelves and books in a truck and installed them charmingly here. An elevator is to arrive next week." It would be installed replacing a now seldom-

---

269   (Ed's note: Not referenced in manuscript)

used dumbwaiter to take her between the first and second floors, and also up to the screened-in airy room on the roof. Youngest Fisher son Gerry was attending to the dismantling of her Chicago, Michigan Avenue home, preparing for a two-day auction, not to include books. Ethel's daughters had also found another nurse/companion, Miss Huggins, with whom Ethel was compatible. In July Katharine Fisher held a small open house of close friends and neighbors to welcome her mother, and to say good-bye to the Logans, who were moving to Montana. Before he came to Winnetka, Illinois, Rae Logan had been first a farmer, then teacher, then Superintendent of the Flathead and Crow Indian Reservation in Montana. Frances, continuing the family interest in politics, soon became head of Montana's National Democratic Women's Committee.

Ethel had earlier asked her daughters to take what books from her library they specially wanted, and she had donated others to selected organizations, such as books on philosophy to the University of Chicago and on teacher training to the Graduate Teacher Training School in nearby Winnetka. She now asked Katharine Fisher to write to her fifteen grandchildren, asking what sort of books and topics would interest them. Katharine followed her wishes, enclosing duplicate lists of sets of books and topics, asking the grandchildren to return one list with their 1st 2nd and 3rd choices. Meanwhile, Ethel wrote her granddaughter (this author) about how she was fitting back into a family life. She was pleased that her arthritic hands were gaining some strength; she could even use a saw to help Walter and son Roger, home on vacation, dispose of dead wood from an old tree. She enjoyed settling in at the Fisher household. She helped Katharine pit and store cherries for later canning, played anagrams frequently with Walter Fisher, spent much time in her conveniently-located library and enjoyed her longtime habit of occasionally playing double solitaire.

Groundbreaking of New Healy Building at IJR

The final public event Ethel Sturges Dummer attended, on October 21, 1952, was the groundbreaking for what would become the William Healy Residential School, to be part of the Institute for Juvenile

Research. She joined Dr. Healy, then 85, and his wife Dr. Augusta Bronner, the Institute's first psychologist, at the outdoor ceremony for the new building. It would include an assembly hall named in honor of Mrs. William F. Dummer. During the ceremony Mrs. Dummer presented the Certificate of Incorporation of the Juvenile Psychopathic Institute, as it was originally called, to Welfare Director Fred K. Hoehler. In 1917, the Institute had become placed under the direction of the Department of Public Welfare.

In her talk, Mrs. Dummer described the beginnings of the Institute and the important role played by people such as Jane Addams, and Julia Lathrop, who became Chairman of the Board of Directors. "Another name to remember is John H. Wigmore, who was Dean of the Law School at Northwestern University. He showed from the first keen interest in Dr. Healy's work and when *The Individual Delinquent* was published, he took it at once as a textbook for the course on Criminal Law. The more than forty years that have passed since the Institute was founded have fully justified our early hunch - that a wise physician was as much needed in the Juvenile Court as a man trained in the law."

A letter from Illinois's Governor Stevenson, unable to attend the event, was read. It said in part "When Dr. Healy and his colleagues were working hard to improve services at the Institute and the courts in Chicago, Dean Roscoe Pound, for many years, Dean of the Harvard Law School, said 'The establishment of the Institute for Juvenile Research in Chicago is the greatest advance in judicial procedure since the Magna Carta.'" [270]

Memorial Service

On Sunday, March 7, 1954, memorial services were held for Ethel Sturges Dummer at the Institute for Juvenile Research. Katharine Dummer Fisher welcomed the large group attending. "My sisters and I are very happy you are here with us this afternoon. We feel this meeting is not so much one that marks the end of mother's physical life as it is one which marks the going on of her ideas and influence...We are very

---

270   The Welfare Bulletin, Ill. Dept. Of Public Welfare, Nov/Dec. 1952

grateful to have this place to meet together and we are very grateful for the continuity from the beginning of the Institute until today. She asked Dr. Raymond Robertson, Superintendent of the IJR, to read a message that came from Dr. Healy.

"A wonderful human being has passed from among us. Some have been recognized as worthy notable individuals because of a practical accomplishment, some for the ideas they have cherished and promulgated, some for endearing socially valuable characteristics. Few indeed have been so notably endowed with those combined achievements. Ethel Sturges Dummer was eminently one of the few. Whence came this happy and effective blend? Partly, no doubt, from nature and partly from nurture, but very probably most largely from her long practice of self-discipline in assimilating wisdom from a wealth of sources. These led her from the way of Lao-tse to apply the logic of earth and water to the English theory of George and Mary Boole...She felt herself to be a mystic... in the best sense of the term ...one who somehow is a recipient of spiritual inspiration...Enticed as she must have been to give herself largely to great thoughts, "she kept her feet on the ground as she gave freely to herself and her support to practical and planned adventures in exploring, in dealing with, human needs."

"Not professionally trained, she nevertheless had an outstanding appreciation of what science did in fact contribute and can contribute to education, knowledge of the springs of human behavior. It was this and her exercise of what she called her catalytic personality that brought together in 1917 the idea of four leading scientists in the little book *Suggestions of Modern Science Concerning Education*, still valuable reading." He vouched for her service to the world in making possible establishment of the first child guidance clinic, and being farsighted enough to ensure the first five years be devoted to research.

Mrs. Fisher commented: "Mother had many friends. They touched her on many different aspects of life. Among all these many friends there were some who seemed to have a very special sympathy and understanding of what mother meant, how she thought, what she did and why she did it." Mrs. Fisher went on to say that she and her sisters had chosen two from among their mother's many friends to speak and give a balance of the many sides of their mother's life: Miriam Van Waters who worked with their mother for many years when she was active in the practical kinds of things, and Milton Singer, who knew her in later years, when she seemed concerned with philosophy and the meaning of things, ideas and faith.

Excerpts of Van Waters' remarks follow:

"From every experience I think that I ever had in Mrs. Dummer's company, both in her presence and in half a lifetime of correspondence, her eye was on the far horizon as well as keeping a keen perspective on the foreground and middle ground." ... "The unique thing about talking with Mrs. Dummer was that she took your idea without controversy, almost without question, lifted it and sent it winging some place. You always went away with some development, not only within you but in your thoughts."

"Mrs. Dummer, having launched a program, gave no backward look. There were no instructions. Her ideas were creative, which gave a remarkable freeing and releasing of the spirit."...I came to Mrs. Dummer's house in Chicago many times. It is very important to note the people going up and down stairs of a person's house. On that second floor library you would meet janitors and school teachers and college presidents and research workers and famous scientists, or those who were going to become famous, carrying books, bringing books up and back down. Like Jacob's ladders were the stairs of Mrs. Dummer's house at 679 North Michigan Avenue. Then one would ask what it is that is the essence of the creative process. I think it is recognition of thoughts in others and personal qualifications in others that are going to serve the ties; and I feel so very strongly, having worked for government all these years, that the maintenance of our country, the salvation of our country, resides in the volunteer who has social invention in her mind and the good will and the skill and the resources to carry it out...When we get combined with that compassion, awareness, a keenness of what government has set up and what government is doing, confidence in the scientific process, then you have indeed a pioneer in social invention."

"The important thing I think", about all of the people who received support from Mrs. Dummer, "is how she related us one to the other. There was something in her that had respect for science, yes, but she was never taken in by it...Over and over again, when people came up to talk things over with her, we found she was better read in our particular field than we were. There were the books, and they weren't there just to mellow on the library shelves. They were in her mind and she could discuss them. She could use the vocabulary of the scientist, but she was never fooled, never taken in, by our pretensions because she balanced them always with philosophy, with poetry and with her own intuition. She believed there were one world of thought and one world of feeling in spite of all the conflicts, all the departmentalizing. There was a continuous building up of a greater understanding and a greater harmony in this art of thinking which alone she believed could supply the basis for right feeling."

"So let us say integration is one of the components of creative experience; and let us say prodigious industry is another, because she certainly had that. Let us also say humility because Mrs. Dummer's humility was a humility beyond humility. It had a basis. It had as basis serenity. Just as she always released others in conversation, so she herself was released. No need for self-protection, no need for self-assertion; she was at home in the eternal, really, to a most remarkable degree.

"Thus we have in the creating components faith, serenity, relatedness and humility. I think we also have a cosmic patience, the kind of constructive composure that was never more apparent to me than when I would tell Mrs. Dummer some of my political vicissitudes, both in California and in Massachusetts. I think she felt that even politicians could be saved; even they were human."

"Always it was Mrs. Dummer's family. ... (She) never did speak of herself. It was always the grandmother who was asked a question and 'grandmother said'. There is always before us, scientists and social workers in the field of our troubled American scene, the demonstration of a family where Mr. Dummer and Mrs. Dummer jointly created ideas and methods for the education of children…Without any "I" in her make-up, without any doubt or fear or belief in death, Mrs. Dummer lived her life fully.

Mrs. Fisher then introduced Dr. Milton Singer, who described how he was working on problems in the history of modern logic from George Boole; when he met Mrs. Dummer on the way to a meeting he happened to be carrying George Boole's "Laws of Thought".

"From that point began an intellectual association which not only illuminated many of these technical problems which troubled me a good deal, but which brought me, I think, to see something of this philosophy of life which Miriam Van Waters was giving you a glimmering of, but I think a very vivid glimmering.

"First, I realized there was a very profound method of thought and a profound philosophy of life embodied in George Boole's work. From that point on I gradually discovered that Mrs. Dummer was more than she seemed. She always, it seems to me, very unobtrusively hid behind these many books, many authors, many people who had come into her life, whom she had brought together; so that one was not inclined at first, if one were somewhat academic, to find the mind and admitting spirit behind this shell. …I found that she had read many, many more books than I had, and she constantly called to my attention books in my field that I did not know. But what shocked me most of all was that she had a way of reading these books, a way of thinking about what she read, that went beyond the particulars and beyond the academic problem".

For example, she had obtained a copy of George Boole's early textbook *Differential Equations,* full of mathematical symbolism beyond his mathematical capacity. In two weeks he received ten pages of notes and equations from Mrs. Dummer that went right to the heart of the problem. It was an example of how she said her mind works like a magnet.

"When she read a book it would somehow in an uncanny way impart to her thoughts that were nuggets ... of real thought, of wisdom; and the rest she let go. Beyond this personal way of intuitively reaching the truth I found that there was a very profound philosophy of life." One of her tendencies that struck him most of all was her quality of patience – based on a very deep understanding of life's rhythms and on the love of other people...I think it was this same patience which led her into that capacity to understand the essence of diverse religions.

"I know no one will think it disrespectful if I say that Mrs. Dummer was fun to know. She had an unfailing interest in people as well as ideas, and she was encouraging and stimulating as a friend...Her astute remarks on current happenings and personalities were often a delight and she maintained a refreshing objective judgment...But there was no complacence in her attitude. She faced the intellectual and historic events of her long lifetime with a discerning eye and wove them one by one into the fabric of her personal faith only after she had studied them carefully. ....She had a philosophy of life that had given her a full and happy life."

Katharine Fisher closed the gathering by telling the guests about something her mother had said a number of times, and again when they were talking about the life she had. She had said, "Mother, it has been a wonderful life, this pattern that you have woven of so many diverse threads, so many different threads, so many colors, with the pattern repeating, the pattern varying and making a various patterned design; it must be a great satisfaction to you." Mother gave that bright look and said, "It has been a wonderful life, hasn't it?" Then she added, "But I am not the weaver; I am the shuttle."